Unite

Forgotten Worlds, Volume 6

Prudence MacLeod

Published by Prudence MacLeod, 2023.

UNITE

by

Prudence MacLeod

Copyright 10/13/2019

UNITE

First edition. November 29, 2023.

Copyright © 2023 Prudence MacLeod.

ISBN: 978-1927478271

Written by Prudence MacLeod.

A Curse From the Past

"You are certain none remain?"

"None, sir. The entire system has been cleansed of all resistance. A few scattered bands of fugitives are all that's left."

"Then set out the auto defenses, full perimeter. No one, no species must ever discover what evil was wrought here. The knowledge they possessed must perish with them."

"Yes, sir, destructors deployed, observation posts manned. If any species comes here, they will never leave."

"Very good. Set course for home."

Grounded

"Approaching the next star system, Admiral. Eighteen planets, four in the Zone. Probie reports plenty of space junk, all ancient, nothing under power."

Suvi-jean Sorenson, admiral of the small fleet of ships holding the last humans alive in the galaxy, nodded and turned to the small alien woman across the table. "Looks like you're clear to go, Captain Morthel."

Smiling brightly, she rose to her feet and snapped off a salute. "Thank you, Admiral. I'll prepare my ship." Jeannie smiled as she watched the Earalithian woman hurry away.

In ancient times, the Earalith ruled a vast empire containing thousands of star systems. Morthel was one of only eleven Earalith still alive. No longer a shy, introverted minor princess of a royal family, she was now the energetic captain of the fleet's main explorer ship, EX2.

Morthel arrived at her ship, Explorer Two, EX2 as they called her, to hear the sounds of a crying baby. "Crew all aboard?"

"Crew is aboard, Captain," replied SUVI 13, the ship's main surface explorer and bodyguard. All SUVI (survivor of unknown viral infection) have enhanced abilities and use the number of their survival instead of a name. This man was the thirteenth survivor.

"Lock her down. Three, request launch."

"Ship is locked down."

"We have launch clearance."

"Take us out, Three. Aim for the nearest planet in the Goldilocks Zone, then hit it."

"Aye, Captain, launching. Target acquired; ship is underway."

"Thank you, Three." The baby was still crying, so Morthel turned to her security officer, Connie Kim. "Want a break?"

"Thank you, Captain. I have no idea why she's fussing."

"I do," said Morthel, as she accepted the child from her mother's arms. Earalith have two thumbs on each hand, and little SUVI 21 loved it when she got to wrestle with Morthel's thumbs. Morthel held the baby in one arm and wiggled her thumbs, which were immediately grabbed in tiny fists. The child stopped fussing and giggled. Since the birth of Twenty-One had proved the SUVI can reproduce, bearing children with SUVI abilities, the SUVI had been confirmed in official records as a species in their own right.

"You just want to hear the captain make funny sounds, so she'll be embarrassed in front of the crew, don't you?" cooed Morthel, as she played with the child in her arms. "You're just trying to make me lose all respect and my reputation as a fierce captain." The child was laughing now and wrestling with those agile thumbs.

"Approaching planet One, Captain."

"Thank you, Three." Morthel's next sentence was lost in the frightened wail of the baby in her arms. Her eyes snapped back to the child for only a heartbeat. "Dammit. Shields!"

The shields went up just as the first salvo hit the ship. Further fire was erratic and scattered as a shielded ship is nearly impossible to target. "Get us on the ground! Find a spot where we can inspect for damage."

As the agile ship dropped toward the planet, her captain turned back to the child in her arms. She was quiet once again. "So, you're another intuitive, like Eighteen and Twenty, are you? Good to know."

"Captain?"

Morthel turned to Connie and Thirteen, the baby's parents. "Twenty-One is SUVI, as we know, and I believe she's fully intuitive. She was fussing because she sensed danger. I was able to distract her for a while, but her sudden cry of alarm clued me in. She's quiet now, so I'm guessing the immediate danger is past." She rose and handed the baby back to its mother.

"Where are we, Three?"

"Flying over ruins, Captain. There's an open spot up ahead, could have been a space port at one time. Possibly a good place to check for damage."

"Sensors, anything moving?"

"Just us, Captain, and no other life signs."

"All right, Three, set her down. How's the atmosphere?"

"Looks breathable, Captain."

"Good to know. Commander Peters."

"Captain?"

"Care to babysit our youngest crewman while the rest of us check for damages?"

Lilly Peters, the ship's botanist, chuckled at that. "Sure, why not? There's nothing growing around here anyway. "Come to Aunt Lilly, Twenty-One. We'll hang out on the ship while Mom and Dad keep the engineers from being eaten by giant predators."

"Not funny, Lilly," grumbled Thirteen. "I've still got scars from planet Stormy and those damned predators." He swept the huge scatter blaster to the ready position and Connie opened the hatch. He leaped through with Connie right behind him. "Anything?"

"I've got nothing."

"Me neither. Looks clear, Captain." At his call, Morthel led her pilot and engineer out of the ship. They were followed by the six maintenance personnel assigned to the botanist.

After a thorough inspection of the hull, followed by full diagnostics of all systems, EX2 was given a clean bill of health. "Looks like we're good, Captain," said the engineer. "EX2 is tough all right. We took one direct hit, but the shields kept the rest from making contact."

Morthel noticed the man never took his eyes off the hull of the ship and seemed nervous. "Thank you, Brodie. All right, people, everybody back aboard. Thirteen, speculate, what happened?"

"Looks like this place is another dead planet, Captain Morthel. Offhand, I'd say they were at odds with somebody from somewhere else. I think we triggered another ancient planetary defense system. Whatever it was, it didn't try to follow us down."

"Our shields worked well," said Connie. "Maybe whatever it was is still up there looking for us."

"And maybe it turned away expecting something else down here to take over," sighed the engineer, Brodie Cortez. "There's no way to know for sure right now." He was still looking down at the ship's deck.

"So, do we return to the fleet, Captain?"

"Not yet. We're here to explore the planet, so we'll continue that mission. Lilly, see if you can raise the Reacher for me."

"Aye, Captain. EX2 calling Reacher, come in Reacher. EX2 calling Reacher, please respond."

"Reacher here, EX2. Rerouting you to Admiral Sorenson." A moment later Jeannie's voice reached them. "Sorenson here. What's up, Morthel?"

"We were hit by some sort of planetary defense system, Admiral. We're on the ground, but unharmed, the shields worked well."

"Do you need assistance?"

"Not at this time, but perhaps we've awakened something that could become a problem if there are more in the area."

"Understood. I'll ask Sessas to look into it. Sorenson out."

"Three, take us up and begin a standard grid search pattern. Brodie, keep those shields up just in case."

"Aye, Captain, shields are raised. Captain, do you believe it's safe to proceed?"

"I do. As you can see, our early warning system is sleeping peacefully." She was smiling at the baby in Connie Kim's arms.

Two hours later they found it, a vast city that spanned half a continent. Much of it had given way to the vegetation that was reasserting itself over the planet.

"Lilly, you on sensors?"

"I am, Captain. I've got plenty of life signs, but not seeing anything that looks truly organized. I'd say that the people who built this city are long gone, and the natural world is taking over."

"Any signs of automated defenses?"

"Sensors show no active power sources. SUVI sensors are quiet, no immediate threats indicated."

"Good to know," chuckled Morthel. "All stop."

"Ship is stopped, Captain."

"Thank you, Three."

"Captain?"

"Huh? Oh, sorry, Thirteen. Just thinking, that city is massive, easily equal to an Earalith capitol. That tells me there was a lot of tech at work down there at one time, and that would require vast amounts of energy. Lilly, poke around a bit, see if you can see anything that might suggest a generation plant."

"What's on your mind, Captain?"

"Thirteen, my friend, anything that could generate enough energy to run a city of that size would surely be of interest to main engineering."

"It would at that."

"Actually, I'd rather look for something else," said Lilly.

"Lilly?"

"Captain, enough people to fill that city would need a food supply second to none. I wonder, might there be a few remnants of that miracle for us to find."

"Getting ahead of myself again, was I?" chuckled Morthel. "Continue grid pattern, Three."

"Continuing grid search, aye." Morthel smiled as she felt the ship resume its forward motion.

* * * * *

At the end of shift Morthel ordered the ship into low orbit. "Anything on sensors, Lilly?"

"Nothing moving, Captain. Not on the ground, nor in space."

"Thirteen?"

Connie had to nudge him as she seemed lost in thought. "Huh?"

"The captain?"

"Oh, sorry Captain. No, nothing on SUVI sensors, neither mine nor the baby's."

Morthel sat beside him and spoke kindly. "What is it, Thirteen? What's eating at you?"

He sighed deeply and did not meet her eyes. "I didn't see it coming. That's my job, and I didn't see it coming."

"Nobody did," she replied. "Your special talent is possible futures, not sensing out hidden dangers."

"Maybe, but I should have. When we moved close to the first Earalith colony I sensed the danger, why not here?"

"It's worth noting," said SUVI 3, "that neither of the truly intuitives, Eighteen and Twenty, nor the admiral herself, sensed it either, or we'd have been forewarned. Don't beat yourself up over this one. We got down without a scratch, could have been worse."

"Yeah, I guess."

"So, take a look and see if we get out of here alive." That voice came from Ensign Brodie Cortez, an engineer on his first exploration trip. He had been so eager, Morthel had taken him on, but his tone caused her concern.

Thirteen's voice was cold and dangerous when he responded, sending a shiver through most of the small crew. "Was that an order?" As a former slave to Brodie's people in their underground colony, Thirteen didn't respond well to that tone.

Brodie shrank away and turned to the sensors. Morthel patted Thirteen's arm. "Easy, my friend, easy. Actually, that might not be a bad idea, but it can wait a few days, we've got a lot more to do before we start worrying about going home.

"Get some rest everyone. Three, Axel, Connie, and Twenty-One will take the first shift with me. Lilly, you and the rest get the second shift."

As Brodie headed for the sleeping quarters, Connie, baby in her arms, stepped in his path. "You're not in the Caverns now; best not to annoy a SUVI." She stepped away to the engineering station. "Shields at full, Captain."

Morthel looked up, saw Connie glance at Brodie's retreating back, then nodded. "Thank you, Officer Kim."

Thirteen stopped to kiss Connie and the baby goodnight. "Leave him to me," she whispered. "I'll handle it." He nodded and continued on to the sleeping booth. As a former slave, he'd had a strong reaction to the young man's tone of voice. He was a bit annoyed with himself for rising to the bait so easily.

The ship was on auto and those awake gathered near the pilot's station, talking softly to let the others sleep. "Three."

"Yes, Captain?"

"I have no idea at all of a slave's experience, but I do have plenty of experience on the other side of that coin. Have I ever used that tone with any of you?"

"You're the captain," chuckled Alec Hoff, crew chief of the maintenance people, "all captains sound like that."

"I'm serious, Alec. Three?"

"No, Morthel, you haven't."

Morthel looked thoughtful for a moment. "Antha would say we're two sides of a common coin, you and Thirteen from slavery and me from royalty. No matter the species, I'm sure there are similarities in the manner of interactions. Those times are long past for all of us. Three, if you ever hear me speak like that to any of the SUVI, any of the crew for that matter, tell me immediately."

"Captain?" Three grinned. "It would be unseemly for a pilot to chastise the captain."

Morthel chuckled at that. "Just say, 'Captain, flip a coin,' and I'll get the message. Yes, as captain I have to give orders, but there's a right way and a wrong way to do it. I watched Vice-Admiral Drake when she was captain, and I try very hard to follow her example."

"Captain, nobody on this crew has an issue with your style of command, or the fact you were promoted to captain. You're good and we all have full confidence in you."

"Thank you, Three."

Connie smiled. "Captain, you and Thirteen were friends before your promotion, and he's more than happy to see you in the role. Believe me, there are no issues here. He's just messed up a bit; he didn't sense the danger before it happened.

"No, ma'am, the problem here is Brodie. He was a baby when they landed on Elysium and spent all his life in the caverns working beside his father. He's a good engineer, but the open spaces are freaking him out. I doubt he's even looked outside the Reacher before coming aboard this ship. Hard not to look from EX2."

"Seriously?"

"Connie's right," said Alec. "I noticed him shaking when we left the ship to inspect for damage. I'll bet he had no idea this would happen and is totally freaked out by it."

"Thank you, Alec, I didn't notice that, and I should have."

"You can't catch everything, Captain. That's what you have us for," smiled Connie.

"All right, but let's keep an eye on him."

"We will, Captain, and I'll keep a reign on Thirteen as well."

"Good luck with that," chuckled Morthel.

Field of Obstacles

Next morning, while EX2 continued her search, the rest of the fleet hung back, just outside of the planetary system. They knew the defenses they'd triggered ringed the entire zone of this area. It wasn't meant to destroy them, simply to drive them back. Once they got past it, the system would now prevent them from leaving, ever.

All the fleet captains, plus the chief engineer of the Reacher, were gathered in the captain's briefing room. "Rhonda?"

Rhonda Moore, captain of the Reacher, sighed as she replied to the admiral. "It covers half the system and is especially dense around the four planets in the Goldilocks Zone. It appears to be fully automated and programmed to attack anything that approaches.

"Morthel was a bit eager to get to the task, and she went in fast. She actually reached the first planet before the system responded. Since Probie, our super probe and advanced scout, is small and probably didn't approach any of the Zone planets too closely, she didn't trigger it."

The rest of the captains sitting around the table nodded their agreement. All their sensors told the same story. The admiral seemed to be lost in thought and her partner, the Vice-Admiral, Amanda Drake, smiled and gently patted her arm. "Jeannie?"

"What? Oh, sorry. All right, we have EX2 stranded down on that planet with no way home. From the size of that defense system, we can surmise all four planets were colonized, and that there could be plenty of salvage to be had, but first we have to get our people back. Is there any further word from Morthel?"

Amanda smiled as she gazed at the small tablet in her hand. "Message just in. They're fine, still flying grid and finding extensive ruins. No sign of danger. Apparently, once you get past the defenses, the planet is quite peaceful."

"So, what's our next move, Admiral?" asked Sheila Singh, captain of the Orca, the fleet's war ship.

"Tell me that the defense system is completely automated."

"All our sensors say it is," said Sheila.

"All right, then we have here the possibility of salvage and much more, but we're blocked by an ancient defense system. Will our shields stand up to that system?"

"They will, Jeannie," said the chief engineer for the fleet, Moira Duncan.

"Okay, then we need a plan to neutralize that system."

"Is easy," came a metallic voice. Captain Sessas, a Saurian, communicated primarily through a translation speaker. In spite of her language difficulties, she had risen to captain of the fleet's main rescue ship, and her ever practical nature always earned her respect.

Suvi-jean smiled at her earnest friend. "Tell us, Sessas. How do we take that system down?"

"Retriever go down fast to help EX2. Robots chase, Orca shoot down, more come, F1, Orca, small ships, EX4, Reacher, Kreenon, join in, Retriever turn back, fight too. Target practice for Sheila crew."

"Oh yeah, I like that plan," grinned Sheila.

"You humans are all crazy," sighed Jeannie. "We SUVI do our best to keep you alive and all you do is go looking for more trouble. Sessas, you're as bad as the rest." Everybody smiled at the Saurian woman's hissing laughter.

"All right, let's give it a shot." The admiral reached for her comm. "Sorenson to Nine."

"Here, Five."

"Warm up the ship, we're going out."

"I'll top up munitions. Ship will be ready."

The small fighter ships hung in space just outside the Reacher. "All right, Captain Sessas, you are clear to go."

"On our way, Admiral," sang the voice of SUVI 20 as Retriever shot away toward the nearest planet in the Goldilocks Zone.

Jeannie just watched and shook her head as the small ship sped away then suddenly started a zig-zag pattern. Dozens of the defensive robots appeared and began shooting erratically, unable to accurately target the ship when the shields were engaged.

Suddenly the Orca appeared and opened fire. The robots exploded by the numbers, but they still kept coming. Orca spilled out her small fighters, who set to work efficiently. Jeannie nodded her approval, but for every robot destroyed, several more appeared.

The Reacher's main cannon fired, and a long tunnel of clear space appeared in the mass of robots, but still they came on. All the small ships engaged, but eventually they were forced to retreat. Once all ships returned to the edge of the system the robots disengaged and seemingly vanished.

The tired crews headed for the various mess halls while the captains gathered in the Reacher's briefing room. "Everybody's here, Admiral," grinned Amanda.

"Thank you, Vice-Admiral Drake," sighed Jeannie. "Well, people, we learned a few things today, some good, some bad, and we got our collective asses handed to us." There were a few chuckles around the table at that. "Sessas, your assessment?"

There was a hint of a chuckle at the woman's response. "Plenty robots, good target practice. Shields work good, enemy can't target ship. Bad side, too many robots."

"Keep going."

"Robots not try to follow, destroy, just keep away, not allow us to go to planet. Sessas think robots not allow EX2 return."

"Clear and precise as usual, Captain Sessas, and I do agree with your assessment. So, captains, any injuries, fatalities, or damage?"

"Retriever all good," replied Sessas. "Low on ammo."

"Second that," said Hal White, head of Security for Reacher and commander of EX4.

"Same, same," agreed Shiela Singh. "Ship and crew performed admirably, we used up most of our munitions, the shields worked perfectly, and we got outgunned."

"Friendship ran low on ammo, too," sighed Captain Linsey da Silva.

"Sadly, the Kreenon had to withdraw early, Admiral," said K'Ron, acting captain of the Kreenon. "We ran out of munitions."

"Understood," nodded Jeannie. "Be it noted, F1 also ran out of munitions and charge for energy weapons.

"So, here we are. Suggestions, opinions, options?"

"Too many robots," sighed Sessas, "can't shoot down."

Jeannie grinned at her earnest friend. "So, what's the solution, Sessas?"

"Not know, Tentee job to figure out." SUVI 20 and Captain Sessas were close friends and Twenty rarely left the captain's side when on duty.

Everybody chuckled at that. "I see that grin, Sister Twenty. Spill it, what's the answer?"

SUVI 20 smiled as she sat up straighter. "Well, how about we capture one, Moira can dismantle the thing, discover what makes it tick, and then Harlan can build us some more effective weapons."

"Sounds reasonable. There are plenty of disabled ones floating loose out there, but if we try to get close to one the rest will come at us again. We'll have to be quick about this. Sheila, Sessas, Hal, Linsey, will ride shotgun for Recovery One. We'll go first thing in the morning. Everybody get a meal and some rest."

As the meeting broke up, Jeannie grinned to hear Sessas on her comms talking to her second officer. "Kumar, top up munitions, we go again after sleep."

"Aye, Captain," came the swift reply.

On the Ground

Brodie came awake with a start at the baby's wail. He bolted through the door of his sleeping booth and raced for the weapon's panel, but Alec stepped in his path. "Easy, buddy, easy. I'm on weapons, besides, she's just hungry, there's no danger."

"Oh, crap. Sorry."

"Maybe you should ask Tommy for something to steady your nerves."

"Yeah, that sounds like a plan." Red-faced with embarrassment, Brodie returned to the booth and shrugged into his uniform. He could hear the child suckling at her mother's breast. With a sigh, he stepped out and went to the engineering station.

"Are we ready, people?"

"All crew at their stations and ready, Captain," replied Lilly Peters, first officer and botanist of EX2.

"Pilot, resume grid pattern."

"Resuming grid, aye," responded SUVI 3 as the ship moved forward smoothly.

A short time later Lilly's voice was heard again. "All stop."

"All stop, aye. Ship has stopped, Commander."

"What have you got, Lilly?"

"If I'm seeing what I think I'm seeing, Captain, I've got gold."

"On screen." Lilly flipped a switch and the forward screen lit up with a vision of an endless sea of golden grain waving lazily in the breeze. "That could be a big part of that food source you spoke of Lilly."

"That isn't," muttered Thirteen. His keen hunter's eye had spotted movement in the tall grain. "Can you get me a better look at that creature, Commander?"

"Working," replied Lilly, as her fingers flew across the sensor panel.

The scene they watched moved closer until they were looking at a large animal. Moving stealthily on six legs, it closed on a gangly biped that didn't seem to sense its approach. The beast charged forward, but several more bipeds appeared and hurled their spears. The predator fell to the ground, lifeless at the feet of its intended victim.

As the hunters gathered beside the kill, one of them spotted EX2 among the clouds. It waved its arms excitedly, pointing upwards. They all turned to look then, as one, they vanished into the vast field of grain.

"Are they still there, Lilly?"

"Yes, Captain, I have them all on sensors. They didn't go far."

"All right, resume grid, Three."

"Resuming grid, aye."

Morthel turned to see the disappointed look on Lilly's face, and she grinned. "Keep an eye on your sensors. As soon as you see a likely spot to fill your crates we'll set down. Just make sure we're the only ones moving around there before we open the hatch."

"Aye, Captain," sighed Lilly. A short time later she found it. "All stop."

"All stop, aye."

"What have you got, Lilly?"

"The perfect spot, Captain. That river has created an open area in the grain field, probably part of a flood plain. It looks solid enough, according to sensors, and it's open enough to see any danger approaching."

"Like those animals?"

"Yes, Brodie," replied Lilly, "like those animals, or those people, or anything else this new planet might have to throw at us. If we land, you should stay here and keep the engines warmed up, just in case we have to make a fast retreat."

Morthel smiled at that. "All right, Lilly says it looks good, Twenty-One has no issues, Thirteen?"

"Sounds reasonable to me, let's go have a look."

"Take us down, Pilot."

"Going down, aye," chuckled SUVI 3, as the ship settled gracefully to the wide sand bar.

"Brodie, on sensors. Are we alone here?"

Bent over the sensor panel, his voice drifted back to Morthel. "Yes, we're alone."

"That's 'Yes, Captain,' Ensign. Never forget who you're talking to," said Connie.

"Yes, Captain. Sorry."

"Hatch is open," called Thirteen as he leaped through, Connie right beside him. "Clear here. Connie?"

"Clear skies here. Looks good, Captain."

Morthel smiled with delight. "All yours, Lilly."

Eagerly, Lilly Peters led the six maintenance people assigned to EX2 off the ship. They were her labor force, bodyguards, and friends. She'd renamed them "the supers", but they called themselves "the mule team".

Ensign Alec Draven, the leader, took a fast look around and grinned. "That looks like a level spot to place the crates, Commander."

"Just one should do it for here, Alec," replied Lilly.

"You sure? Maybe two, just in case."

"You know me too well."

He chuckled with delight and held up two fingers as the cargo bay door swung open. The crew pulled out two large crates and carried them over as Lilly began harvesting samples from the grain field.

The first crate was barely full when Brodie began shouting. "Get back to the ship, something's coming. Get back here ..."

Morthel, who had come out to enjoy the sun turned back to the ship but bumped into the shields. with a muttered curse she reached for her comm. "SUVI 3, are you on the ship?"

"At pilot, Captain."

"Take control of the ship and lower the damn shields so we can get in. Tommy, are you there?"

"On babysitting detail, Captain."

"Put the baby in a safe place then assist Three."

"Understood, Captain, shields are down."

"Thank you, Lilly, get your people back inside. Thirteen, help me protect their retreat. Connie, get back inside and secure the safety of Twenty-one."

"Aye, Captain," replied Connie.

Morthel turned to see Thirteen facing off against four strange creatures holding spears. "Easy, my friend. We don't want to hurt them if we don't have to."

"Understood, Captain," grinned Thirteen. "Should I try to make friends?"

"Go for it. I've got a blaster at the ready in case your stellar diplomatic skills fail us."

"Hey, I'm not SUVI 20, I can do this." He grinned at her soft chuckle behind him.

By this time, Lilly had her people back inside the ship. She saw Tommy, the medic, with a stunner in one hand and the baby in the other. Brodie was cowering on the floor beside the sensor panel. "Ensign Brodie Cortez, you are hereby confined to sleeping quarters until the captain returns to the ship. Three, what are we facing?"

"There's only four of them I can pick up on sensors. They haven't come any closer."

"Good to know. Tommy, you and Twenty-One prepare the med kit in case we need it. Connie, man the forward guns, Three back to pilot. Alec, tail gun, I'll take a long-range weapon and go back."

"Forgive me, Commander Peters, but since the captain is ashore, you're the commanding officer aboard. I'm the Security officer; I should go back."

Lilly sighed then nodded. "All right, Connie, you go. Mary-Jane, on forward guns."

"Yes, ma'am," grinned the girl as she scurried into the gunner's chair. Connie was already back outside, taking up a position to Morthel's left.

Thirteen had been facing the four beings for some time, but no one moved. "Any time at all, Thirteen."

"Aye, Captain." With his arms spread wide and his hands empty, Thirteen stepped toward the visitors. He barely covered three steps before one raised a spear. Grinning with anticipation, Thirteen balanced on the balls of his feet and readied to charge.

Seeing his change of posture from one of submission to one of battle ready, the creature threw the spear. To his surprise, Thirteen caught it easily, looked it over, tested the point, then tossed it back. Somewhat chagrined, the creature picked up the spear and looked at Thirteen who spread his arms wide and took a few steps to his left, making sure a missed throw would not endanger his wife or the captain.

Furrowing his brow, the spearman took a few steps and launched the spear with all his strength. Thirteen caught it easily, spun it like a baton, then tossed it back. He pointed at the spearman then to another, and then spread his arms wide once again. They both threw their spears, but he caught them and tossed them back.

The creatures spoke excitedly among themselves, then all four lined up to throw their spears. "Thirteen?"

"I'm good, Captain. Let me do this."

"All right, if you say so."

"Show off," muttered Connie.

"Quiet, wife, I'm working here."

Morthel and Connie both chuckled at that as he spread his arms wide to invite the spears. In truth, his armor would prevent any harm should he miss the catch. Four spears flew at him, and in a blur of motion, he caught them all.

Thirteen was about to toss them back when a huge beast charged from the grain field. It leaped at the now unarmed aliens, but a spear thrown with the superior strength of a SUVI hunter pierced its body and it fell dead at their feet. Thirteen approached and passed back the rest of the spears.

All four were staring at him now. Carefully, three accepted the proffered spears, then Thirteen pulled the spear from the dead animal, cleaned it off on the grass, then handed it back to the obvious leader. He held the spear in his hands as he looked at the dead animal then turned back to Thirteen and passed him the spear.

Thirteen accepted the gift, then pulled out a long-bladed knife from his belt and held it out, but the creature didn't seem to know what it was. Thirteen nodded then knelt and began to dress the kill. A few passes of the knife and the alien suddenly understood. This time he nodded, accepted the proffered knife, and set to work. His companions pitched in with stone knives and the work was soon done.

Thirteen gathered up a few pieces of driftwood from the river's edge and Connie produced a fire starter kit from her pack. The alien hunters soon had stones piled up, a makeshift spit set to work, and the meat was cooking.

Through all this, Morthel was talking to them and encouraging them to respond. They were fascinated with her musical voice and the talking box in her hand. They were even more surprised as the box started to make sense. Slowly they began to see that the box was repeating her words so they could understand.

The leader waved his hand for silence then faced Morthel. "You are chieftain here?"

"I am."

"Have you brought your warrior to kill us?"

"No, we don't want to hurt you, we want to trade."

"Trade? What do you need?"

"Food, for one thing. This grain that grows everywhere, if it proves useful to us, may we harvest some?"

"Of course, but why ask, you are powerful, you can take whatever you want."

"Perhaps, but that is not our way. This is your world; we will take only what you give us permission to take."

"You are an honorable people. We are relieved you are not the demons."

"The demons?"

"The lore speakers of our people tell of a time when we were as many as the birds of the air, that vast parts of the land were covered by our homes. The knowledge of our ancestors was great, and when visitors came from the sky, they offered to share that wisdom.

"The visitors became angry when the knowledge was shared, and they began killing everyone. Some of the ancestors managed to hide under the ground and thus the people survived. Since that long-ago time, we watch the sky in fear the demons might return.

"When that which carries you was seen, all the people hid in fear. My three brothers and I volunteered to come see what you were going to do."

"You mean you came to kill us before we could kill you, yes?"

"Yes," he sighed.

"We'd rather be friends," smiled Morthel.

"As would we, safer that way, and more meat."

Her musical laughter brought a smile to his leathery face. "My name is Morthel. May I touch you?"

He pulled back suspiciously. "Why?"

"It is the way of my people to greet a new friend by touching them gently. I won't harm you." He nodded and stepped closer. "You're too tall, you'll have to bend down a bit."

Tentatively, he bent toward her. She reached to lightly grip his shoulders then touched her forehead to his. "I am Morthel of Earalith, citizen of Reacher, Captain of EX2. Speak to me as Morthel."

Gently he returned the gesture. "I am Dour-den, chieftain of Bi-Lad Clan. Call me Dour."

"It's a great pleasure to meet you, Dour," she smiled as she stepped back. "The man you called warrior is named Thirteen. He is a SUVI hunter. His companion is Connie, a human peacekeeper. We are not warriors; we wish no conflict, merely to trade and learn."

"We will trade with you, Chieftain Morthel. Tell me, what is it you wish to learn?"

"We are a curious folk, Dour. We want to learn about your world, about your people, and we wish to learn from the things your ancestors left behind. Will your people permit this?"

"You want the ancient knowledge; that which brought destruction on all our people?"

"No. Dour, when your people were many, covering much of the land with their homes and food sources, they had ways to keep those homes warn, to prepare foods, to do other magical things as we do.

"Our people know how to make that blade Thirteen gave you, and much more. We simply wonder if your ancestors knew better ways of doing things than we do, and if so, can we learn these things to help make our lives better.

"We also would like permission to investigate the places where the ancients lived and worked, to take what is useful to us. We will trade for what we take. Do you think your people will allow this?"

"I believe so. Will you trade knowledge for knowledge?"

Morthel gave no sign, but she was instantly alert. "If possible, I am certain we would. What knowledge would you seek?"

Dour turned to gaze into the flames of the fire and sighed. "The lore speakers tell of a time before the demons came. In that time it was said there were four lands floating on the sky, and our people prospered on each one. After the demons slew most of our people in this land, nothing has been heard of the other three.

"I wonder if those tales are true, and if the other three lands exist. If they do, do the people still live there, are they as great in knowledge as you are?"

Morthel nodded, then spoke softly. "Long ago, my people lived and prospered in many such lands, and we were as the stalks of grain in these fields. Sadly, all are long gone now; only me and a few more remain of the once mighty Earalith. I understand your desire to learn of the rest of your kind, Dour.

"I can tell you this, the other three lands still exist, but at this time I know not if any people survive there. When we came to this place we could see all four lands, but this one is the first we have been able to visit. Our plan is to learn and gather what we can here, then investigate the next one, and then the next until we have learned all we can from these lands. If the great admiral permits me, I will return with whatever I have learned of the others and share that knowledge with you."

Dour seemed lost in thought and she didn't disturb him. Finally, he looked up again and spoke. "You are an honorable people. Will you permit me and one other to accompany you when you visit the lost lands?"

"Yes, I believe that will be possible. I'll speak to the admiral and seek permission."

"Then, when the sun rises, we will return to our home beneath the ground and seek out the lore speaker. She will surely want to come with us as well."

"I would be honored to meet with her. When the day dawns I will contact the admiral and speak with her about these things. In the meantime, do we have your permission to continue taking samples from the ground?"

"Granted, friend Morthel. Sleep well, my brothers will watch the camp."

"Then I will rest easy knowing a friend is watching for danger." She rose and stretched, then called out. "Back to the ship, people, time for a rest cycle."

Phobia

As they entered the ship, Connie reached and took the baby from Lilly's arms. "Shields?" Morthel nodded and Connie threw the switch. "You don't trust our new friends?"

"I do," sighed Morthel, "but I don't trust an alien planet with big nasty predators. Who knows what else is running around out there?" She sank into a chair and indicated the rest should do the same. "Three, what the hell happened?"

SUVI 3 chuckled as she sat near the captain. "I was running a diagnostic on the flight controls and was on the floor on my back with my head under the control panel when I heard Brodie freak out. I crawled out just as you called and ordered the shields dropped, but before I could act there was the sizzle of a stunner, Brodie was on the floor twitching, and Tommy, gun in one hand and baby in the other, was shutting down the shields."

Morthel smiled. "Then what happened?"

"Second Officer Peters appeared at the hatch and took command."

"Lilly?"

"Tommy already had things under control, Captain," replied Lilly. "We secured the ship; Connie took heavy arms and went back out to assist and cover your retreat as necessary; we manned the guns, and I stood by to raise shields if needed."

"Well done, Lilly. What did you do with Brodie?"

"I confined him to sleeping quarters until you were ready to deal with him."

"Again, well done. Bring him out, Alec."

"Aye, Captain." He rose, walked back to the sleeping quarters, and tapped lightly on one door. "Come on out, Brodie, the captain wants a word."

Shamefaced and with downcast eyes, he emerged and followed Alec to the seating area. Morthel rose to face him. "Well?"

"I'm sorry."

Suddenly SUVI 13 was nose to nose with him. "That's 'I'm sorry, *Captain*.' Boy, if you don't start showing proper respect to the captain, I'm going to start teaching you manners. I promise you won't forget the lessons. Now start over and watch your attitude." With that he stepped back.

Morthel had made no effort to hold Thirteen back, she just stood waiting. "I'm sorry, Captain."

"What happened, Ensign Cortez?"

Her voice had an edge to it, and she had addressed him formally. Still looking at the floor, he responded softly. "I was at the sensor panel, Captain. I saw several life signs approaching. I sounded the recall to the ship, raised the shields, then started toward the arms locker."

"Then what happened?"

"He shot me," accused Brodie, as he pointed a finger at the medic.

"Tommy?"

"I had the baby in my arms, Captain, Ensign Cortez was obvious panicking, so, being unable to restrain him with the child in hand, I hit him with a stunner, low setting, then raised the shields so the crew could return to the ship."

"Well done, Tommy. You were cool in an emergency, took the appropriate action, and still protected both the child in your arms as well as the ship's crew. Well done.

"Now, Brodie."

"Yes, Captain?"

"You panicked, stranded the captain and first explorers on an alien planet facing unknown dangers. Tell me, what would you have done if there actually had been a serious threat? Hide here on the ship, leaving the rest of us to our fate?"

"I don't know. It all happened so fast I didn't have time to think, and then he shot me."

Morthel resumed her seat but didn't invite him to sit. "You've had several hours to think this over. Have you come to any conclusions?"

"No." Thirteen leaped to his feet and Brodie took several steps backward. "Sorry. No, Captain."

"I don't believe you, young sir. Try again."

"Yes, all right, I panicked, I'll admit that. It won't happen again, I swear."

"Sit down, Brodie, tell me what's going on for you."

He sat a respectful distance away from her and from SUVI 13, who was watching him closely. "I honestly don't know, Captain. It started when we went out to inspect the ship. I stepped through the hatch and it was like a kick in the gut. I felt exposed, alone, no place safe. All I wanted was to get back on the ship."

"And?"

"None of you seemed to understand the danger, or just didn't care. We watched that monster stalk those aliens, and no one seemed to care, but when I saw all those life signs on the sensors, all I could think of was one of those creatures getting inside the ship." He raised his eyes and looked at everyone gathered round; he felt he had no friends here; they were all against him. He lowered his eyes again and held his peace.

Morthel sighed and settled back into her seat. "All right, Brodie, I get it. None of us knew this would happen, especially not you. Some people just can't handle open spaces, and you've never encountered such a thing before.

"However, it's the way you handled it that disturbs me. From now on you will man the engineering station only. Once we return to Reacher, I'll talk to Captain Moore and see if I can get your old job back for you.

"Okay, rest period. Three, Connie, Alec, Twenty-one, will keep me company for the first watch. The rest of you get the second watch. Sleep well everyone."

To Catch a Dead Fish

Aboard the Reacher, the crews of the small ships gathered for their next foray against the defense system. Olga Volkov, captain of the salvage ship Recovery, looked up to see the chief of security and a young woman approaching. She knew who that woman was. "Commander White?"

"Captain Volkov, as I understand this, Recovery One will make the attempt to salvage a dead robot."

"Correct."

"You'll have to be quick."

"Don't I know it, and mine isn't the most agile ship in the fleet. What's your point?"

"We were thinking you might consider a new pilot for this little adventure."

With a chuckle, Olga turned to the young woman. "Commander Ebony Graves, I presume."

"Yes ma'am," smiled the eager girl. "I'm here to help if you want me."

"EX4's hot shot pilot? Oh, you know I do. Go take the chair; I'm sure Hank will be more than happy to give over for this one."

As the girl hurried aboard Recovery One, Olga turned back to Hal White. "I truly appreciate this, Commander."

"Hal, please, Captain, call me Hal. Yeah, I figured you could use her skills on this one. I'll take her grandfather for this mission. The man's dang good, but not in her league. Got any ideas on how you're going to approach this?"

"I'm wide open to suggestions at this point. How would you approach it?"

Hal chuckled as he turned away toward his own ship. "I'd let Ebony do it."

Olga smiled and shook her head as she watched him go. "Why the hell not?" With that, she headed onto the ship and sought out Ebony at the pilot's station. "Think you can fly him?"

"No problem at all, Captain. Can you tell me how you'd like to approach this? We won't have a lot of time."

"Originally, I planned to follow standard procedures, only a lot faster. However, The chief of security suggested I let you do it."

Ebony grinned. "Yeah, that figures."

"Got any ideas?"

"Well, the fastest way to get one into the hold is to go right at it, throw open the doors, spin about and drop down over it, slam the doors shut and burn for home."

"Think you can do that?"

"Not a problem."

"All right, Commander Graves, the mission is yours. I'll just go down to the cargo bay and warn the crew what you're planning. They can get some netting strung up to catch the flying fish."

Olga was halfway to the cargo bay when Suvi-jean's voice came over the comms. "Sorenson to all captains, are we ready?"

"Orca ready and standing by, Admiral."

"Retriever ready and willing, Admiral."

"Friendship ready Admiral."

"Kreenon is ready."

"Reacher is standing by, Admiral."

"Very good people, F1 is ready. Olga, is Recovery One ready?"

"Recovery One ready to go, Admiral."

"Ebony Graves, is that you?"

"It is, Admiral. I'm at the helm on Recovery One and Captain Volkov has given me the mission. She's a great ship, this should be fun."

"He. All Earalithian ships have male identifying AI. Earalithian ships are male."

"Oops, sorry Admiral, I should have known that."

"Understood, Recovery One. How do you want to do this?"

"It would be nice if somebody could get their attention while I sneak up on a dead one, distract them for a minute."

"I'll take on that job," came the voice of Captain Sheila Singh of the Orca. "I'll go stir up a fuss and you go catch a dead fish."

"All right then," said Jeannie. "We have a go. Orca will go cause trouble, and the rest of us will ride shotgun for Recovery One."

The Orca sped away toward the second planet in the zone. She was soon surrounded by robots with hundreds more converging. "Get busy, Recovery One," came Sheila's voice over the comms.

Ebony's voice then came over the ship's comms. "This is the pilot, hang onto something." With that, Recovery One leaped away, bearing down on a cluster of free-floating derelict robots. A large number of live robots turned toward him, but he would arrive first.

"We're closing in, get those doors open then hang on tight; this will create some G-forces."

"Cargo bay doors open, Pilot," came Olga's voice.

"Acknowledged." With a suddenness that nearly threw the entire crew into free fall, Recovery rolled on his side, the tail swinging about while the nose almost completely stopped dead. There was a great clanging noise then Olga's voice once again. "Target acquired. Get us out of here."

Even as she spoke, the pursuing robots opened fire and the ship shot away toward Reacher, at the edge of the system. Olga made her way back to the command center and took a quick glance at the sensors. With a grin and a shake of her head, she reached for the comms. "Recovery One to Admiral Sorenson."

"Here, Olga."

"Mission accomplished, Admiral, and we just passed the safety zone, pursuit is turning back."

"Understood, Recovery One. Fleet, this is the admiral, mission complete, return to Reacher, all possible speed."

The fleet returned to Reacher to find Recovery One in the landing bay waiting for them. As F1 landed, Jeannie leaped out and ran to

Recovery One where the Chief Medical Officer was busy checking out the crew of the salvage ship. "How many are injured, Carla?"

"Nothing serious, Admiral, just a few bumps and bruises, a few mild cases of whiplash and some motion sickness."

"Mild?" groaned one young woman. "If anyone finds my stomach in there, I'd like it back please."

"Sorry," said Ebony, as she approached the young woman.

"The hell you are," groaned the still dazed girl. "You're a complete savage. My god, we all could have been killed."

Ebony struggled to hide her grin. "I've got a friend who can get us a table at Simple Pleasures. If I suck up and buy you a treat, will you forgive me?"

"Maybe, give it a shot and we'll see."

"With your permission, Admiral."

"Go on, Ebony, you've earned your reward. That was a masterful bit of flying, worthy of a SUVI." Jeannie grinned, as Ebony took the girl's arm and led her away.

"Bit of a rough ride was it, Olga?" asked Jeannie, as she turned to the captain of Recovery One.

"That and then some," was the rueful reply. "I've seen her fly EX4 on maneuvers and had an idea of what to expect. When she said to hang on, we all did. Darn good thing too, or half of us would have been killed."

Jeannie chuckled. "I'll admit it, that maneuver took me by surprise. Did the target survive the capture?"

"I have no idea, let's go ask Moira. She and her crew just hauled it away." Together they headed for Engineering.

Ebony and her companion entered the café and were swiftly ushered to a small table. "Earalithian cake is Ebony's favorite," smiled the server, "now what appeals to you, ma'am?"

"I've heard a lot about that famous cake, but never had the chance to try it. May I have a piece of that too, please?"

"Coming right up," she sang as she hurried away.

"So you're the famous Commander Ebony Graves. I'm Ensign Brie Elliot, ship's medic on Recovery One."

"How about we just be Ebony and Brie? I'm famous?"

"Three days to make Ensign, a few months to make Commander? Yeah, you're famous, some sort of super genius, so they say."

"Wow, and I just thought I was born lucky."

"Lucky? You think you're lucky?"

"You're here with me, aren't you?"

Brie sat back, her mouth forming a perfect O. Suddenly she blushed deeply. "Stop it. You're supposed to be sucking up, not embarrassing me."

"Oops, sorry, my bad."

"Oh you are not sorry either, you're a mean woman."

"I am, I'm a true rotter and I freely admit it."

Brie's sweet laughter brought a smile to Ebony's face as the cake arrived accompanied by a pot of Earalithian tea. "Enjoy, ladies," smiled the server.

"Thanks, Maxi," replied Ebony, as the woman hurried away to another table. A soft groan of delight brought her attention back to her companion. "Well, does the taste live up to its reputation?"

"That and then some."

"So, I'm forgiven then?"

"A part of me wants to say no, but I've been trying to get in here for weeks. The line to get in is always so long I've never made it. Rumor has it they keep one table ready in case the captain or admiral wants to visit. Is that true?"

"We're here aren't we?" grinned Ebony.

"So you're not only famous, but you have friends in high places, too?"

"Not bad for a kid from the Caverns, right?"

"The Caverns? You're from the Caverns, but you're not SUVI, right?"

"That's right. The SUVI lived through hell, especially the women; I just hid in our quarters for fifteen years."

"I don't believe that for a minute."

"It's true, Brie. It was the only way to survive, hide in the quarters and play VR games, study VR programs, and don't let First Prime or his goons see you."

"VR games, is that why you're making all the VR training programs?"

"Yeah, the admiral heard that's how I learned to fly a ship, so she promoted me and gave me a task. I'll be lucky if I finish it before I retire."

"Yeah, tough job, all right. Did you know the admiral in the Caverns?"

"Only by reputation. Everybody knew that one day the SUVI would rise up, and there would be hell to pay. That's why First Prime was so hard on her. SUVI 5 is the greatest of all the SUVI, the strongest, fastest, smartest, and her mind never stops. Gramps always said it would be her to lead them to freedom."

"Yeah? Wow. How do you feel about her being the admiral, really?"

"Brie, I'm utterly thrilled SUVI 5 became our leader. Without her we'd all be dead, killed by the weapon on Earalith Colony 2, or obliterated by the Wrax, or a dozen other possible disasters she's kept us safe from."

"You really admire her, don't you?"

"Shows, huh?"

"Just a bit."

"Oops, looks like we've overstayed our welcome."

"What???"

"There's Sub-Commander Karissa Glenn just entering the kitchen. That means Alli is ready for her break, and they'll want this table. See, here comes Maxi." Ebony rose to her feet, scooped up the dishes and passed them to Maxi who took them as she sped past. Ebony took Brie by the arm and steered her out the side door and onto the grand mall.

"Okay, what now? Want to poke around a bit?"

"Sorry, Ebony, I can't, I have to get back to Recovery One and see what all got destroyed in the medical station, then resupply."

"Oops."

"Not your fault, girl, not really. You had a crazy job to do; you did it and kept us all alive while you did. It was a wild ride, but necessary."

"So, am I forgiven?"

"You fed me cake, of course you're forgiven."

Ebony smiled with delight. "Want to do it again sometime?"

Brie gave her arm a gentle squeeze then walked away. "Absolutely" she called over her shoulder. "You know where to find me." Ebony's smile widened as she headed back to her office.

* * * * *

While Ebony introduced Brie to the magic of Simple Pleasures, fleet captains were in a meeting with the admiral.

"All captains present, Admiral Sorenson."

"Thank you, Vice-Admiral Drake," chuckled Jeannie. "Well people, mission accomplished. While Moira is investigating the treasure, let's have a look at how we did, what we learned. Sheila?"

"Yes, Admiral. I learned that Orca is even tougher than we'd thought, and the magic shields work wonders. Even though they swarmed us, they couldn't target us effectively.

"Downside, they seem to be able to coordinate their efforts. Even though our shields rendered us invisible to their sensors, enough of them bumped against said shields to help the others locate us. One would latch onto the shields and the rest would fire on it. It would be destroyed, but that tactic did weaken the shields."

"Oh, in what way?"

"As it exploded, the power required to maintain protection seriously drained our reserves."

"And there it is," sighed Jeannie, leaning back in her chair.

"Admiral?"

"Nothing is ever perfect, but our shields are close. I've been wondering where their weakness was, and now we know. They draw a lot of energy when under heavy fire. Be aware of that and make sure your crews are aware as well. Too much fire for too long could cause them to fail.

"Olga."

"Aye, Admiral. Well, I learned my ship is capable of a lot more than I thought; and I learned to wear armor when Commander Graves is at the helm."

"Bit of a rough ride?" chuckled Hal White.

"I suspected it would be when I saw the grin on your face, but in truth, Hal, I'm not sure we could have succeeded without her. I only wish the artificial gravity had managed to keep up with the maneuvers. It was a bit tricky, and we nearly lost a couple of crewmen. As is, we had a lot of scrapes and bruises, but we got the job done. Thanks again for the loan of your pilot."

"The Earalith built them tough, all right," agreed Jeannie. "Sessas, your observations?"

"Shields draw plenty power, yes, but not main problem."

"Oh?"

"Tentee say."

SUVI 20 sat up straighter as she spoke. "We noticed the power drain almost immediately, but I could see they're communicating with someone somewhere. Yes, they coordinated the attack, but Orca was well out of sight behind the gas giant when we approached with Recovery One, yet they were already on their way back to intercept us.

"There's a central observation post directing them from somewhere in this system. We need to find it and knock it out. We also need to know what frequency they're using to communicate and jam it."

"A central observer is directing them? Are you sure, Twenty?"

"There were none within the line of sight when we launched, yet they were on an intercept course."

"Damnation," muttered Jeannie. "That's good work, Twenty. All captains point your sensors everywhere; find everything and anything that might hide our observer."

"I believe I may know where it is, Admiral," said KaRon.

"You do? How?"

"It's the Maccay, Admiral. They are utterly inquisitive, always pointing the sensors at this and that, and they've spotted a large asteroid on the far edge of the system that doesn't want to conform to the laws of physics. It keeps making small course changes; changes that could put it in a position to observe us from a distance."

"Have Captain Grill send those coordinates to Retriever. Sessas, go blow that thing to hell and back."

"We go," came her reply along with her hissing laughter. SUVI 20 was already on the comms to the Retriever's crew.

Once again, the diversity of the fleet's crew had proved its worth. Suvi-Jean smiled.

The Mystery Deepens

While the fleet went fishing for a dead robot, Morthel contacted the Reacher and spoke with the Vice-Admiral. "Morthel, Amanda here, Jeannie is away on a mission. How can I help?"

"We've got a couple more days of exploring here, Vice-Admiral, and we've encountered a sentient species. Thirteen managed to make friends with them."

"Thirteen?"

Morthel laughed at that. "Yes, they're hunter/gatherers, they have lots in common. Amanda, they told me some of their mythology, and they understand their species once inhabited other lands. I believe they mean the other three planets in the zone. They asked to accompany us as we visit those worlds, to see if any of their kind have survived there.

"Do I have your permission to proceed?"

"Absolutely. Morthel, before you try to leave that planet, check in with us first, we may have a bit of trouble getting you home."

"Understood. Morthel out."

As Morthel turned away from the comm station, Thirteen stuck his head back inside the ship. "Dour is back with the lore speaker, Captain."

"Coming."

Morthel stepped outside to see a group of people standing back, curious, and a tall female standing beside Dour, and leaning slightly on a staff. The woman was as tall as Thirteen, but rail thin, her chocolate brown skin glowing in the morning sun. Her upswept ears twitched slightly as her deep purple eyes took Morthel's measure.

"This woman is Goranan, Lorespeaker of our people," said Dour, as he backed away leaving the two women facing each other.

Morthel took a step closer. "It is an honor to meet you, Goranan. May I touch you?"

"Dour has spoken to me of this," she replied in a rich contralto voice that was soon translated by the box on Morthel's belt. "You may touch me." Goranan bent at the waist slightly so Morthel could reach her.

Gripping the woman's shoulders gently as she touched their foreheads together, Morthel spoke. "I greet you, Goranan Lorespeaker. I am Morthel of Reacher, captain of EX2, the explorer ship behind me. Speak to me as Morthel."

Goranan passed her staff to Dour then gripped Morthel's shoulders. "I greet you, Morthel of Reacher. I am Goranan of the Duraden People. You may call me Goranan or Lorespeaker as you choose."

As Morthel smiled and stepped back, Goranan spoke again. "Tell me, Morthel, why have you come here, and from where did you come? There is no mention of a people such as you in the lore of the Duraden."

"We came from a place far from here, Lorespeaker. No other of our kind has passed this way before. We people of Reacher are a wandering folk, just trying to survive. When we found your lands, we came down for a closer look, to see if we might find useful things here, and perhaps new foods to try."

"You are welcome to whatever you might find useful. Dour said you know of the lost lands."

"Yes. As I understand your history, there were four lands occupied by your ancestors. We know their locations and plan to explore them."

The lore speaker paused then sighed. "Morthel, the lore of our people is twofold. The elder lore, now considered no more than the imaginings of the elder people, says that the four lands are round objects hanging in the sky and circling the sun. Great was the power of the elder people, and when others came from afar, they shared the ancient wisdom.

"The strangers became angry and sent demons to kill all the people. It is said that the demons still haunt the skies between the ancient lands. Most believe the elder lore is nothing more than a mythology.

"The younger lore is the story of how the people began deep inside the caverns and grew stronger and wiser as they moved higher through the tunnels to hunt in the sun under the open skies. This is more a history of our people."

Morthel nodded. "Walk with me, Lorespeaker." She led the woman inside the ship. "Goranan, I believe your Elder Lore to be true. This land, although it appears flat, is actually shaped more like a closed fist, floating in the sky while circling the sun. The other three lands are the same.

"Let me show you." She flipped a switch and a three-dimensional model of the system appeared over the sensor panel. "This one is the land on which we stand, far away are the others, this one, this one, and this one.

"What you call the demons, attacked us in the sky as we arrived here. My people believe they will try to prevent us from leaving. However, we're determined and even now my people are working on a way to stop the demons. Once they tell me it is safe to travel, we will visit these other three lands, and you are welcome to accompany us."

"This is a map of the trails to the other lands, a map of the trails through the sky?"

Morthel nodded. "Yes, we are here, Reacher, our home, is out here beyond the demons. When we go we will go first to this ..." She was interrupted by the comms.

"Admiral Sorenson to Captain Morthel."

"Here, Admiral."

"We've captured one of the robots; Moira is working on a way to neutralize them right now. Are you safe where you are?"

"All is well here, Admiral. We'll be fine."

"Excellent. We'll let you know when it's safe to return. Sorenson out."

"That one is your chieftain?"

"Yes, that was Admiral Sorenson, our supreme leader, she who commands us all."

"Her voice speaks of great strength, of a controlled power, and command."

"Yes, Admiral Sorenson is the greatest of us all. Hopefully I'll get a chance to introduce you. Have you ever journeyed to the place where your ancestors dwelt in the great cities?"

"No, but I have longed to do so. Each Lorespeaker must make that journey once, but the taracks have grown numerous, and the path is too dangerous. I could find no one to accompany me for protection on the journey."

"We could take you there in this ship, well above the ground and quite safe from the predators."

"You would do this?"

"Gladly."

"There is a private ceremony I must perform. The night will come and pass away again before I am ready to take the sacred journey."

Morthel smiled and nodded. "Then we will continue our explorations and return to this place when the sun rises tomorrow."

With that, she led the lore speaker back out into the sunlight. They were in time to see an act that could destroy the budding friendship between their peoples.

Connie had just passed the wailing baby to Thirteen when he heard the grunt behind him. Clutching the child to his chest, he squared his shoulders to protect the child, as well as his wife, as best he could. The spear lanced through the air to shatter against his armor, causing him to take a staggering step forward.

As the spear shattered, Connie drew her blaster and fired. The young Duraden hunter who'd thrown the spear was hurled through the air to tumble in a heap several long paces from where he'd stood. The baby was back in its mother's arms and Thirteen had the spearman in his hands before Morthel stopped him with a single word. "Hold."

Thirteen froze with his hand around the man's throat. "Connie, is Twenty-One hurt?"

"No, Captain."

"Thirteen, are you harmed?"

"Negative, Captain."

"Will anyone here speak for the man who threw the spear?"

"Captain Morthel, I'm his chieftain and his father, I must speak for him. May I talk to him first to learn why he threw the spear?"

"Thirteen?" The SUVI nodded, never taking his burning gaze from the man in his grasp.

Dour approached carefully. "Ravel, why did you attack our new friend? What madness possessed you to do such a stupid thing?"

"It wasn't an attack," choked out the man. "Always he catches the spear, no matter from where it is thrown. I wondered if he could do it from behind."

"Did you hear, Captain Morthel?"

"I heard, Dour, thank you. Thirteen, do whatever you think is just."

All the Duraden gasped at that, the Captain would not interfere. She had judged the foolish youngster as guilty and now his fate rested in the hands of the mightiest hunter any of them had ever seen, a man he had just attacked from behind.

With one hand, Thirteen shifted his grip to the man's rough tunic and held him off his feet with one arm. When he spoke, his voice cut like a knife. "Hear me well, one and all. The next one to attack me, or to put my companion and child in danger, will face my full wrath. Mary-Jane, you on guns?"

"Affirmative," came the response from the ship.

"That stone," said Thirteen, pointing to a large boulder slightly to his left. A beam of light lanced out from the ship and the stone was sliced in half. As the Duraden backed away, their eyes wide with fear, Thirteen thrust the hapless man away from him, then turned and walked back to Connie and the child.

Morthel stepped forward. "I assume that demonstration will be sufficient. We wish to be friends with the Duraden, but you must understand, attacking us would be foolish."

"Captain Morthel, what will happen to that man now? What will your warrior do to him?"

"Nothing, Lorespeaker. The man made a foolish mistake, and Thirteen has pointed out the error of such an act. No further action will be taken, your man is free to go, and my offer to carry you to the great city remains."

"You are a good and just people," replied Garanan. "I will return to this place at sunrise tomorrow to begin the journey."

"We will meet you here, Lorespeaker." With that, Morthel turned away and returned to EX2. "Back to the ship everyone. We still have work to do. Lilly, have you finished here?"

"I have, Captain."

"Three, take us up, resume grid search."

"Resuming grid search, aye." The ship rose into the air and moved swiftly out of sight of the Duraden.

Later that day, they flew over yet another great city in ruins and, beyond that, a forest that was trying to reclaim the land. "I've got life signs on sensors, Captain. Looks like a hunting party of Duraden."

"Is there a likely place to set down, Lilly?"

"Not really, Captain."

"Then on we go."

A while later Lilly called out from the senor panel again. "Ship all stop."

"All stop, aye," came Three's response.

"What have you got, Lilly?"

"Another major grain field, Captain, but this looks like a different plant."

"Any likely landing spot nearby?" grinned Morthel.

"Forty degrees left, six hundred meters, Captain."

"Hover over that spot, Three."

"Aye, Captain." The ship moved off to hover above the bare patch of ground that appeared to be about three times the size of the ship.

"Lilly?"

"No life signs nearby, Captain, and the ground appears solid. Looks good."

"Take us down, Three. Twenty-One, you and I will hold the ship while Thirteen and Connie clear the area."

Chuckling, Connie passed the baby to Morthel then reached for her armor. The ship settled gently to the ground then Thirteen threw open the outer hatch. Connie leaped through with him close behind. "Looks good to me. Thirteen?"

"Agreed. Looks good, Captain."

"All yours, Lilly."

"Thank you, Captain. Alec ..."

"Two crates?"

"Two crates," chuckled Lilly.

Several hours later the ship rose to continue her explorations. Lilly was smiling with delight. She had samples from two new grains, and plenty to start production should they prove viable. Meanwhile, if the grains were useful, they could harvest plenty from the open fields leaving time for hydroponics to get a second crop on the go.

A Useful Weapon

While Morthel and crew were catching a rest before the meeting with the lore speaker of the Duraden, the crew of Retriever was in a game of tag with the robots. "Oh-oh," came SUVI 20's soft voice from the sensor panel of Retriever.

"Tentee?"

"We've got company, Captain Sessas."

"Company?"

"Looks like that thing has figured out that we're coming after it. It's taking evasive action, and all of the robots are on our trail."

"All?"

"Yup."

"Is good. We let them chase, EX2 escape planet. Billee, on guns?"

"Aye, Captain. On forward guns."

"Fire when ready."

"Aye, Captain."

"Whoa, that thing is coming right at us," exclaimed Twenty. "He's going to try to blow past us. Get him, Billy."

"Target acquired."

He opened fire with all he had, but the object began to evade. As the pilot brought the ship around, SUVI 20 opened fire with the tail guns. The object tried to evade her fire and came into range of the forward guns once again. It exploded just as the pursuing robots caught up.

"Full speed, open space."

"Aye, Captain," came the terse reply as the pilot brought the ship around and headed away from the system.

* * * * *

"Bridge to Captain Moore."

The rest of the captains and the admiral were still in the briefing room. Rhonda reached for her comm. "What is it, Anita?"

"Looks like every robot in the system just went after Retriever. Retriever is headed for open space, pulling the robots after her."

Jeannie sat up straight and pointed at Sheila Singh who leaped to her feet and fled the room. "Anita, this is Admiral Sorenson. Get me the Retriever."

"A moment, Admiral. Retriever, this is the Reacher, acknowledge."

"Retriever."

"Go ahead, Admiral."

"Sessas, what the hell are you doing? Where are you going?"

"Far away, let them chase, then use star drive to get home."

"Wait, Jeannie, this is Twenty. They're falling back, going dormant. I think they need to be close to the star for energy. We're too far out and they're powering down. We'll circle around a bit until they're all dead then we'll come home."

"Sounds good, Twenty. The Orca is on her way to cover your retreat. Did you get the leader?"

"Got him, Admiral. Blew his ass to Mars ... Mars is a small planet near Old Earth."

Jeannie sighed and shook her head, grinning. "I know what Mars is. You'll pay for that, SUVI 20, now make sure those things aren't coming back to haunt us, and then come home."

Everyone smiled at the laugh in her voice. "Aye, Admiral. Understood."

At that point the admiral's personal comm pinged. "Sorenson."

"Moira here, Jeannie. We've cracked the codes on these robots. We can now shut them down and issue them any commands you wish."

"That's the best news yet, Moira. Sessas has managed to draw them out to the edge of the system. Apparently, that causes them to power down and become useless."

"Aye, that's a bit of good news. Would you mind terribly if we salvaged a few?"

"Salvage? What for?"

"Metals. We can melt them down into sheets of usable metal, glean a few useful spare parts as well."

"I'll ask Rhonda and Olga to drop by and you can make a plan."

"Understood. Engineering out."

"Anita, get me EX2 on the comms, please."

"A moment only, Admiral. Reacher calling EX2, respond."

"EX2 here."

"I have the admiral for you, EX2."

"Morthel here."

"Morthel, we seemed to have solved the robot issue, it's safe to come home now."

"With permission, Admiral, I'd like to stay another day. We've promised to carry the lore speaker on her sacred journey to the forgotten city. I'd also like to bring her with me when I explore the next three planets in the Goldilocks Zone. She's already given permission to take whatever we find useful from this planet."

"Granted, Morthel, I'd like to meet and talk with this lore speaker, as would Linsey, I'm sure. Take whatever time you need."

"Thank you, Admiral. Morthel out."

"Well, Morthel seems to have good things in store for us, Sessas and Moira have solved the robot issue, I think we can safely call it a day. Get some rest everyone."

Lorespeaker's Journey

Back on EX2, Morthel sighed and resumed her seat. "Well, I'm about ready to call it a success and get some rest. Lilly has her crates full, and it looks clear for the salvage crews to take over in the cities. I just want to see where Garanan wants to go and make sure we mark that area as hands off."

"We should just go home," muttered Brodie, but Thirteen heard him.

"Just one more day, Brodie. You can hide in your quarters if need be."

Brodie glared at him, but Thirteen didn't back down. "Boy, you're your own worst enemy. Everybody on this ship would be more than willing to help you if you'd put that attitude in your pocket and let us. Yes, something unusual happened to you, I know what that's like."

"What would you know about it?"

"I watched as a fever killed thousands of my people, then realized I'd been infected. I knew that, even if I managed to survive, I'd end up a slave."

Brodie hung his head and didn't make eye contact. "Point taken. You win."

Thirteen sighed and relaxed his posture. "It's not a contest. When things like this happen there are no winners, only survivors. You've got a bad case of agoraphobia and didn't know until it was too late. How could you have known, you spent your whole life in the caverns, and then inside a ship.

"We'll get you back there. Once inside you'll be able to return to work and live a useful life, just know your limits and stay inside."

"Know my limits. So, what are your limits?"

Thirteen sighed and relaxed his posture. "My temper for one, and a clear knowledge that, should I ever cross the line, I'd have to face SUVI 5. That's not high on my priority list of fun things to do."

Brodie gave a slight grin and nodded. "Yeah, what would you say are my limits?"

"The agoraphobia and the resentful attitude. We're not your enemy, Brodie, the disease is."

"And once I'm back on the Reacher I can never leave?"

Thirteen chuckled at that. "As prisons go, it's pretty comfortable."

In spite of himself, Brodie started to relax. "Easy for you to say, you can come and go as you please."

"Not really. Don't forget, I'm SUVI, we're group oriented, herd animals, we need other SUVI close by or we freak out. Every ship in the fleet with a SUVI on the crew has at least two, except for Friendship. For some reason Eighteen handles it better than the rest of us. Twenty nearly went bat-shit crazy a dozen times when she and Jake White were marooned on Stormy. I won't even tell you what shape Eight was in that time he got lost in a storm on Elysium."

"So you do have a weakness."

"Far too many, Brodie. The key is to be aware of them, and work around them. An example for you is to stay focused on the engineering panel until we get you back inside the Reacher."

"That and keep my mouth shut?"

"It's a start," grinned Thirteen, as he turned back and sat beside Connie.

"Can I ask what you stay aware of, what you work around?"

Thirteen sighed and relaxed deeper into his seat. "I see futures, possible futures, all the time. The key is to keep my trap shut and trust people to do their jobs. Every time someone makes a decision the future changes.

"I did as you suggested and looked ahead. Had the Captain decided to risk the return to Reacher when you had that episode, we'd never have made it. However, the captain didn't ask my advice, and I forced myself not to offer it. She made the right decision without me sticking my nose into her business.

"That's not the first time I've held my peace with Morthel as captain. I trust her to make quality decisions, decisions that affect me and my family, she never disappoints. You see, Brodie, I understand your attitude because I battle that same demon, but I trust these people, my crew mates, to do their jobs. They're good at what they do."

Brodie just nodded and Thirteen went on. "It was different in the caverns, everybody was out for themselves, you didn't dare to trust, that's why we have to try harder, you and I."

"Yeah, I guess. It does make sense at that. Thanks." Thirteen nodded and Brodie returned to his engineering station.

When everyone settled down for the night, Thirteen was on the first watch with the captain. "I didn't know that about you, my friend," she said, as she settled into the seat facing him.

"What, that I see possible futures all the time?"

"Yes, that. How do you manage to function?"

"It's not quite what it sounds like," he chuckled. "I have to consciously ask myself, if I do this what happens next? If we go here, what happens next? It's a survival thing, a gift from the virus. To a plant eating creature living in a vast herd on a planet it would be a handy tool for continued survival. For a space faring explorer, it can be somewhat tricky.

"For example, if I ignore Brodie, or worse, keep getting on his case for his attitude, his resentment could cause him to do something stupid that would endanger us all. Then it gets fuzzy from there. If he accepts my help, then he could end up in a far better situation and so would we. All up to him now."

"You knew we couldn't get back, but you didn't speak?"

"Morthel, if you couldn't work that out for yourself, then you'd never have made captain."

She chuckled at that. "Thanks for the vote of confidence, now tell me what else you're not telling me."

"I don't entirely trust the lore speaker."

"Oh? Why not?"

"Can't say, it's nothing I can put my finger on, nor is it anything I can see, but it's there."

"Yes, I did notice the baby getting uneasy when Garanan was here. Take another look, see if anything pops up."

He nodded then closed his eyes and drew a deep breath, and then another. She sat patiently waiting until he opened his eyes and sighed. "Nothing concrete, but there is a danger associated with her, not from her directly, but connected to her somehow."

"Then we'll honor our promise but stay alert as well. I don't want another experience like when the robots attacked and drove us deep underground on Colony Three. Alert the others, but not Brodie, he's nervous enough as is."

"Understood," he nodded.

* * * * *

The next morning, the Duraden were waiting at the campsite when the ship settled to the ground and the hatch popped open. "Greetings, friend Captain Morthel," Garanan said formally. "It is traditional for the lore speaker to be accompanied by two companion/guardians. Is this acceptable to you?"

"It is friend Garanan."

"Then our clan chieftain, Dour, and his son Ravel shall accompany me."

"Right this way," smiled Morthel, as she stepped aside to allow them access to the ship.

As they entered, the young Ravel kept his gaze firmly on the ground. It was he who had thrown the fateful spear at Thirteen's back.

"Please, sit here," said Morthel, as she indicated the seating area. "Here is a map of the city as we saw it from above. Is there a particular place there you wish to visit?"

"From the time I was young I have recited the pathway to the sacred place," replied Garanan, "But I have no idea how to find the way from the sky."

"You've never been there, but you know of certain landmarks to search for, yes?"

"Yes. As we approach the endless land of ancient homes, a tall building with a rounded top that shines in the sun should appear."

"All right, the city is north-east of here. We'll start with that. Three, head north-east, slow down as we reach the city and look for a tall building with a metal roof."

"North-east, aye." The ship rose into the air, reoriented herself, then moved away at speed.

"Easy now, Three, we have guests."

"Aye, Captain, going easy." There was a soft chuckle from the pilot's chair as the flight smoothed out. "Approaching abandoned city, Captain."

"All stop. Lilly, are you getting anything on sensors?"

"I've got your building, Captain, and a lot of life signs."

"Life signs?"

"No Duraden, Captain, just a lot of animal life."

"Okay, Lorespeaker, what do we look for now?"

"From the building the way is clear. From the building for two hundred long paces walk, then turn to the left and go a hundred more."

"Lilly, show us what's down there."

"Forward screen, Captain."

The screen flickered to life, showing the empty litter strewn streets below. "There," said Thirteen, "that way. You can see the debris has been cleared away to make a path. See, it goes for about a hundred eighty meters then turns left for a hundred more." The trail stopped at a low building that was still standing.

"There is sanctuary for the night," said Garanan. "When the sun rises, walk to its face for a hundred paces then the way to the temple will appear."

"Okay, east is that way," mused Morthel. "Take us another hundred meters east, Three. Let's see what we can find."

"Going east, Captain. Intact building, dead ahead."

"There it is," said Garanan. "I must go inside alone. My guardians will remain outside to make certain I am not disturbed. The sun will rise again before I return. Friend Morthel, you have fulfilled your promise. Will you still be here when I return?"

"We will, Lorespeaker Garanan, for we have also promised to carry you to the lost lands to see what has transpired there. As well, our Admiral has expressed interest in meeting you. When you return to us, we will take you to Reacher and then to the lost lands."

"Then I go to fulfill my destiny." With that, she stepped toward the hatch. Morthel opened it and all three Duraden stepped out.

Garanan approached the door of the building. "I, Garanan, Lorespeaker of Bi-Lad clan, come to learn of the ancient ways." To everyone's surprise, the doors swung open, and she stepped inside. The doors closed behind her, and the two men took up a guard post on each side of the entryway.

"Lilly, did you get anything on sensors from inside?"

"There's a power source nearby, Captain, and lots of live tech operating, but I have no idea what it is. We needed more time."

"Understood. Is there anything else on sensors now?"

"I've lost Garanan and the tech inside the building, but there's several life signs approaching. All animal."

"Throw the shields up around the two guards as well."

"Shields deployed, Captain."

"And now we wait. Alec, you on comms?"

"Aye, Captain."

"Get me the Admiral."

"A moment, Captain. This is EX2 calling Admiral Sorenson, please acknowledge. EX2 calling Admiral Sorenson, please respond."

"Sorenson here, what's up, Morthel?"

"Looks like we won't be getting home until tomorrow, Admiral."

"What's happened now?"

"The lore speaker's ceremonies take longer than expected. The planet still looks good, and we have full permission to salvage whatever we want. Admiral, our current coordinates seem to be a place of importance for the Duraden."

"Mark them well and send them on. We'll leave that area untouched. Good work, Morthel, I'll look forward to meeting your guests tomorrow. Sorenson out."

All was quiet and Garanan returned the next morning. It was easy to see on her face that she was in shock. The two warriors conferred with her for some time, then escorted her back onto EX2 then the ship rose gracefully into the air. "Three, set course for Reacher, it's time to go home."

"Heading home, aye Captain. Course laid in and ready, Captain."

"Garanan, are you all right?"

"I have learned much, friend Morthel, and I will need time to adjust. Much of what I knew is not, and much I did not know has been revealed."

"Do you still wish to visit the Reacher and the three lost lands?"

"Yes, now more than ever."

"Hit it, Three."

"Engaging drive, aye." The agile ship leaped toward the open sky.

"Garanan, watch here," said Morthel, as she flipped a switch, and the forward screen came alive. They could see the city fall away below them then eventually the land and finally they saw the planet hanging in space. "As you have just seen, the Elder Lore was correct; the land is indeed a ball hanging in the sky."

Morthel adjusted the controls and they saw a small pinpoint of light in the darkness of space. "This small light is Reacher. Watch now as we draw closer, it will grow in size until you can see how large it truly is."

Amazed, they watched as the light drew closer, becoming an object, and then growing until it was the massive ship that was home to the entire fleet. Another ship half as large was nearby. Excited and half frightened, the Duraden watched as the huge ship swallowed them up then EX2 settled, and the hatch opened.

Morthel led them out of the ship to where a group of people were waiting to greet them. The lore speaker met the eyes of the woman at the forefront and shivered. This one had to be the mighty admiral the great hunter Thirteen feared, SUVI 5.

"Welcome back, Captain Morthel. I see you've brought guests."

"I have, Admiral. This woman is Garanan, Lorespeaker of Bi-Lad Clan, this man is Dour-den, the chieftain, and this man is Ravel, son of Dour-den. This woman is Admiral Sorenson, the supreme leader of our people, this woman is her companion and second in command, Vice-Admiral Drake, this is Captain Linsey da Silva and her companion, SUVI 18, and this is Captain Moore of the Reacher."

"I am honored to meet all of you," said Garanan, "especially you, Admiral. May I touch you?"

"You may." At that, SUVI 18 gave the admiral a look and received a nod of acknowledgement.

Garanan reached to grip Jeannie's shoulders and touched their foreheads together. As she gently pulled Jeannie toward her, the young Duraden, Ravel, acted, driving a stone dagger for Jeannie's back. Without flinching, she easily caught his wrist and snapped it, causing him to drop the weapon, howling in pain. Thirteen was on him in a heartbeat. "That's a strange form of greeting, Lorespeaker."

Her face pale as a ghost, Garanan backed away from the admiral. "I beg you, do not harm the boy, he only obeyed my direction."

"There is much to learn here, Lorespeaker. Thirteen, take the boy to Carla and get him patched up."

"I'd rather kill him."

"I know, but first we learn what's going on here, then we make such decisions."

"Right you are, Five. Come on, you; let's go get that wrist fixed." With that, he took Ravel by the arm and led him away.

Jeannie turned to Dour. "I expected the blow to come from you, not the boy."

"I was forbidden, great Admiral. The task fell to my son, but he was reluctant."

"Follow me, both of you. Amanda."

"Meeting of the captains?"

"Yes. Call Miriam as well."

"On it."

When all had assembled in the Reacher's briefing room, Jeannie stood to speak. "I am deeply disturbed. While on the planet below, Captain Morthel encountered a species who call themselves the Duraden. Two of them are here in this room.

"Morthel held out the hand of friendship, and has demonstrated our good intentions, however, when I was introduced to the representatives of the Duraden, a few moments ago, they attempted to take my life. They failed.

"Now, Lorespeaker, you will answer my questions truthfully. If you lie, Eighteen will know." The woman's eyes darted to Eighteen and back to Jeannie. Those glowing amber eyes caused her to take a fearful step back, but she bumped into someone. It was Thirteen. He pushed her back toward Jeannie, his eyes glowing amber as well.

"Why did you command the boy to kill me?"

Garanan trembled in fear of the power she sensed from this warrior. Thirteen had said he was a hunter, and that she was the warrior.

Garanan could now see the difference. "I had no choice, great Admiral, the gods commanded it."

"Explain."

"Each lore speaker must make the journey to the home of the gods once in her lifetime. The predators are many and growing more so. Because of this, many years passed and no one would make the trek with me as guardians.

"I felt a great hope when Captain Morthel agreed to take us in her magic ship. We made the trip with ease, and I anxiously approached the doors and spoke my name. The doors opened and I was admitted to the inner chamber. I may say no more of what happened there."

Jeannie took a step toward her, and she gasped in fear. The admiral's eyes were nearly red now and she trembled with the effort of holding herself in check. "You will tell me all of it, Garanan, for if you refuse me, I will go to that temple myself, smash in the doors, rip down the walls, and face your gods in person."

Garanan sucked in her breath at that. "No, please." Her shoulders slumped in defeat. "I will tell you, but I know not how they will punish me for it."

"Begin."

"Inside is a tunnel of stone and light. At the end is a darkened room which speaks as you enter. It asked my name, my purpose, and how I came to be there. I gave my name and said I was there to learn the ancient lore, the unspoken knowledge that brought the doom of the demons upon us. All lore speakers must learn this from the temple so the truth of it remains pure, not distorted through time with the telling and retelling. Once learned, it must never be spoken."

"Go on."

"When I spoke of how I had come there, the voice was joined by others. They became excited, fearful, and demanded to know more. When I said Captain Morthel would show me the lost lands and that

I would meet the supreme ruler of her people, they became more terrified and commanded that we kill you.

"At first I questioned the wisdom of this, and was offended that I was being commanded to betray one who had demonstrated peaceful intentions, someone who had accepted us in friendship. They said they would release the gray plague of death on all the clan should I fail.

"That plague is too horrible to contemplate; it killed most of my clan when I was a child. There was no other choice; I agreed to obey their commands. Dour had already made the exchange of brotherhood with Thirteen and so I was forced to choose the boy to deliver the blow."

To Garanan's astonishment, Jeannie's eyes began to return to green, and she turned away. "Sit down, both of you. Eighteen?"

"She's told you the truth of it, Five, at least as she understands it."

"Agreed," sighed Jeannie, as she sank into her own chair.

"Amanda, your assessment?"

The Vice-Admiral turned to Dour. "Tell me, do your people make offerings of food to the gods?"

"Yes, of course."

"Tell me how that works."

"Three beasts hunted per season are placed upon the ancient altars below the ground. Fresh kills are offered, and they disappear in the dead of night."

"Are there other clans and do they also make sacrifices?"

"Yes, all the clans bring food to the gods."

"As I suspected. Jeannie, I think some of these people survived whatever disaster struck down their civilization. Some retain the old technology while others have returned to a simpler way of life. In the beginning they were probably the hunter/gatherers, supplying food for the techies hidden away. Over time they became two different peoples, one serving the other."

"That makes sense," mused Jeannie. "The thing is, I'm curious why they want me dead."

"They probably think you're one of those who destroyed them in the first place, the ones who set out the robots," mused Captain Baris, Jeannie's grandfather. Jeannie nodded her agreement.

Amanda turned to Garanan again. "Can you tell us the history of your people?"

"Once the people were as the grass in a field of grain, we were so many. Four rich lands were filled with our people and great was their knowledge and understanding. Visitors came from the skies and the ancestors welcomed them, offering to share the knowledge. The visitors became angry and slew the people, placing guardian demons in the sky so we could never regain the forbidden knowledge.

"The four lands were separated, never to reunite, and the minds of the people diminished and fell into darkness."

"I wonder," mused Jeannie. "Could these gods be something else? Are they perhaps the descendants of a guardian outpost that once demanded tribute from those who survived the slaughter?"

"That's a possibility," agreed Amanda, "but if so, why send Garanan to kill you? Would they not welcome a relief ship?"

"Unless they already knew we had defeated their robots and they understand we're strangers," said Rhonda Moore, Reacher's captain.

"In which case, they're probably fearing repercussions," said Sheila Singh.

"Ah well, something to puzzle over another time. Morthel, is the planet ready for salvage operations?"

"I believe it is safe, Admiral. Garanan has already given permission and Lilly's got full crates."

"Good to know," chuckled Jeannie. "Go have a look, Olga. See what you can find useful. Morthel, head out to the next planet and check it out. Take Garanan and her guards with you."

The lore speaker's eyes widened at that. "We're not to be killed?"

"No. You were forced to commit an act of treachery, but the blame falls to those who commanded you. Give me your word there will be no further trouble from you."

"I swear it to you, great Admiral. There will be no further plots against you or your people from the Bi-Lad."

"Eighteen?"

"I believe her, Five."

"Accepted then. Meeting adjourned. Captain Sessas, I want a word with you about this running off into open space."

Morthel led her charges out of the room and back to the waiting EX2. As soon as they were gone, Jeannie turned to Sessas and SUVI 20. "As soon as Morthel is safely on Planet Two, take your strikers down to that temple and tear it apart, find whoever is in there, what tech they have, then we'll decide what action to take. F1 will ride shotgun for you, if you're outgunned, we'll lend a hand."

"So, we're not leaving their temple untouched?"

"No, Twenty. They gave up that right when they sent an assassin for me."

"Understood and agreed, Admiral. Let's go top up the ammo, Sister Sessas."

A Second Chance

Morthel and her party arrived back at EX2 to find Brodie waiting at the hatch. "I'm truly sorry, Brodie, I didn't get a chance to speak with Rhonda. I can put you on leave ..."

"Captain, wait, please. Give me another chance. I can beat this thing, I can, I have to ..."

"Brodie?"

"Captain, I can't spend the rest of my life hiding inside the Reacher. What will happen to me if we find a planet to colonize? No, I've got to get past this, to be able to function. Give me another chance, please."

Morthel glanced past him to Thirteen, who nodded. "All right, Brodie, we'll give it another shot. Just stick to your job and don't try to take over the ship."

"Yes, ma'am. Thank you, Captain." With that, he stepped aside so she and the others could enter.

Brodie headed for his station but stopped beside Thirteen. "You heard?"

"Yes."

"You said everyone on the ship would be willing to help me, does that include you?"

"It does."

Brodie sighed and nodded. "Thanks." He stepped to his station.

Lilly stepped up beside him. "Everything good here?"

"Huh?"

"The ship, is she ready for service?"

"Oh, sorry ... Commander. Yes, engineering is all good and the ship is ready to sail."

She grinned and patted his shoulder. "Ship is ready to sail, Captain Morthel."

"Understood. Three, take us out, destination Planet Two."

"Planet Two, aye. We have launch clearance." The ship rose and slipped from the belly of the Reacher then shot away toward Planet Two.

* * * * *

Once EX2 was well away, Retriever, followed closely by F1, shot away towards Planet One. "How do you want to do this one, Captain Sessas?" asked the leader of her strike force.

"We do Tentee style," she replied.

"Twenty style?" asked SUVI 20, arching an eyebrow at her friend.

"Hard and fast. Strikers, suit up. Tentee, forward guns, shoot door."

"Aye, Captain," chuckled Twenty, as she settled into the gunner's chair.

The ship came in fast and the doors to the temple were shattered under missile fire before the ship settled to the ground and the hatch flew open. Five heavily armed strikers leaped out and sped through the destroyed doors.

The leader snapped on a light exposing the corridor, it was empty. At the end they found a solid metal door. He slapped an explosive against it and turned away. The door buckled inward but didn't open.

"Rayla, got a laser cutter?"

"I do," she replied as a beam of light leaped from the object in her hands, slicing easily through the damaged hinges. The heavily armored woman stepped forward and kicked the offending door aside.

The lights they carried illuminated a stark room with a crude altar. Closer investigation showed them the speaker and receiver system built into the structure. The leader reached for his comm. "Billy to Retriever."

"Report," came his captain's reply.

"The place is empty, Captain. Nobody home. There's a comm system rigged to the altar, whoever that woman talked to isn't here."

"Long range comm or short?"

"A moment, Captain. Rayla?"

The woman poring over the electronics sighed and straightened up. "Long range, Billy. They could be anywhere."

He nodded. "Captain, the comm is long range. The senders could be anywhere in the system."

"Understood. Set bomb, come home."

"Acknowledged." He nodded and his companions gathered their gear, Rayla set the timer on an explosive, then they followed him back to the ship. As Retriever lifted off again, an explosion ripped through the building they'd just vacated. It was utterly destroyed.

On Retriever, SUVI 20 had contacted the admiral on F1. "It was a long range comm system built into the altar, Jeannie. Whoever they are, they were operating remotely, could be anywhere in the system."

"Dammit. Ah well, that would have been too easy. Did they get the frequency used?"

Twenty glanced at Rayla who nodded. "We got it, Jeannie. Rayla is transmitting it to all ships now. If they start up again, we'll know."

"Well done, Retriever. You go find Morthel and ride shotgun for EX2, I'll send EX4 down to keep an eye out for Recovery One.

* * * * *

As EX2 approached Planet Two, Garanan spoke to Morthel. "Friend Morthel, what will the great Admiral do to us now? How are we to be punished?"

"She won't do anything to you, Garanan, you are not to be punished. If that was her intent it would have already happened. No, she understands you had no choice, and she bears you no ill will."

"I will admit, as soon as we got close to her, I knew we would fail. I could feel the power in her and knew; I only hoped we would die swiftly and not be tortured. To find such forgiveness in one so powerful is surprising. We can only hope to find a way to repay her generosity."

Morthel chuckled. "Garanan, the mind of a SUVI works in strange ways, especially the admiral, but always with a purpose. She always has good reasons for everything she does."

"You admire her greatly."

"I do, for it was she who ordered me returned to life."

"Returned to life?"

"Long ago, even before the time of your people's destruction, my own world suffered an event. Almost everyone fled, and those who were left behind died of the deep cold. My most cherished and I lay in our frozen embrace for untold ages until these people found us. SUVI 5 ordered us returned to life and here I am."

"Then your people are truly gods."

"No, my friend, we're not gods, just people with different skills, different ways, but still just people, even the SUVI." Morthel turned to the young guard. "How is your arm?"

"It feels fine, see, I can move the fingers easily. The healer said to leave this on for two more days, but it feels as good as ever."

"Leave it on," smiled Morthel. "It may interest you to know the woman who fixed your arm is the same woman who returned breath to my body. Trust in her wisdom."

"Approaching Planet Two, Captain."

"Thank you, Three. Shields."

"Shields, aye," replied Lilly.

"See anything nasty sneaking up on us, Lilly?"

"No, Captain," chuckled Lilly. "Looks quite peaceful."

"Good to know. Did you bring more crates?"

"Of course, Captain. We have eight empties just waiting for action."

"Then let's go down for a look. Three, begin the standard grid pattern."

"Captain Morthel, is this one of the lost lands?" asked Dour, as they watched the planet grow on the forward screen."

"Yes, Dour. Watch now and we'll get a lot closer then begin our inspection. First, we'll do a fly over of the whole land, see what we can see, then we'll go down and have a closer look."

"You are careful hunters," he nodded with approval.

* * * * *

For two long days they watched the screen, seeing vast devastated cities and endless fields of grain. Forests, fields, mountains, valleys, and oceans passed beneath the ship, but they found no life signs anywhere. On the third day they landed.

"Atmosphere is breathable, Captain."

"Any life signs?"

"None, captain."

"Thirteen, you have a go."

The hatch flew open and he leaped through, Connie right beside him. A moment later her voice carried back inside the ship. "All clear, Captain."

"All right, Lilly, do your thing. Twenty-one and I are going out for a bit of fresh air." With that Morthel, baby in arms, led the Duraden outside. "Garanan, I'm sorry we couldn't find any signs of your people here."

"It's enough you have brought us here, friend Morthel. Perhaps we will encounter more people on the next land. Some must surely have survived somewhere."

"Perhaps you're right," agreed Morthel, as she passed the baby back to its mother. "Let's see how Lilly's doing."

As they approached Lilly stood up and sighed. "Put 'em back on the ship, Alec. We've already got several crates of this stuff."

"Lilly?"

"This is the same grain we found on Planet One, Captain. I've got plenty of samples already. I guess we should check out the cities, see if there's any salvage there for Recovery to play with. Nothing of great interest here for me."

"You sound disappointed," said the lore speaker.

"I am," chuckled Lilly. "I was hoping for different things here, you know, different plants, different things your ancestors might have traded for. Honestly, to support such a vast population as those cities would indicate, a variety of foods would be needed."

Just then Brodie's voice came over the comms. "Life signs approaching, hundreds of them, Captain."

"Sound the recall, Brodie. Leave the shields down until I get there."

"Yes, Captain," he sighed, and she grinned as the siren to recall everyone to the ship sounded. Once all were aboard, the ship rose into the air. The forward screen showed a small herd of large herbivores moving slowly and a pack of predators stalking them.

"Keep us over that herd for a while, Three. If there are any hunters here, we should see them nearby sooner or later."

They didn't, the only life stalking the herd were animals. EX2 moved on to the nearest city. They chose an open spot and the ship settled to the ground. "No life signs, Captain."

"Thank you, Lilly. All right let's go take a look around. Brodie, you and Three inspect the forward sensor array."

Brodie looked up; his eyes wide with fear. Slowly he nodded. "Yes, Captain." Reluctantly, he stepped away from the engineering station and followed Three to the hatch. Thirteen and Connie were already outside, and Lilly was babysitting.

SUVI 3 stopped at the hatch and spoke softly. "Keep your eyes on the ground, Brodie. The trick will be to keep the sight lines short. I'm pretty sure the captain chose this landing spot for the density of the buildings. Keep the sight lines short and you'll be fine."

"Sure, thanks." She led him outside and to the forward section of the ship. A minute inspection that took over an hour confirmed what he already knew, there was no problem. "Everything looks good to me."

"And to me," she replied. "Let's get you back inside the ship."

To her great surprise he said no. "Not yet. I see the captain in that open space over there. I'll go report that all is well."

"You sure you want to do that?"

"Hell no, but she gave me the assignment, probably to make me leave the ship to see what I would do. I need to beat this thing, I'll go report. If I panic and run away screaming, you catch me and drag me back."

"Count on it," she chuckled, as he squared his shoulders and walked toward the captain who was chatting with Thirteen and the Duraden.

"The thing I don't understand," said Thirteen, "is what happened. There were plenty of signs of warfare on Planet One, but not here, yet Planet One has survivors and nothing at all here."

"Germ warfare," said Brodie, as he approached. "That's what took out most of us on Elysium."

"You could be right about that," mused Morthel. "The fighting broke out on Planet One, but they attacked with safer methods on the rest, dropping pathogens from space. What's on your mind, Brodie?"

"Forward sensor array in perfect working order, Captain. Inspection complete."

"Thank you, Brodie, well done. Return to your station aboard the ship."

"Aye, Captain." He turned and hurried back to the ship, sweating profusely, fighting himself to not break into a run.

Morthel turned to Thirteen. "Well?"

"You were right, Captain. Landing in tall buildings where the sight lines are short allowed him to go outside. He was struggling, but he fought it and survived. Have to admit, I'm impressed. I expect he'll never like it in the open, but he'll be able to overcome it enough to function."

"That is my hope. Now, Garanan, you told the admiral that the gods threatened to release a plague, what can you tell me about that?"

"It is called the grey plague of death. The body sickens, becomes weak, bleeds from unusual places, breathing becomes difficult and then impossible, the person dies. Any who were near the sick become so as well. It came to our clan when I was a child. The lore speaker of that time fled with as many as it was safe to take, the rest remained and perished."

"And your gods threatened to release it against your people."

"Yes. Since we failed to kill the great admiral, they will have released it and now the people will be infected. All will die. Friend Morthel, you must warn your people to avoid contact with the Duraden."

"Thirteen, take a look ahead, would you please? Connie, return to the ship and report this to the admiral."

"Aye, Captain." Both people turned away and returned to the ship. As they did, Thirteen made a strange salute and grinned.

"Once again you demonstrate your friendship and trust, Captain Morthel," remarked Garanan. "Even though you know we tried to kill your admiral, still you remain with us with no protection to demonstrate your trust. I must ask why, why would you trust us now?"

"What you did, you did for your people, reluctantly, as it is against your nature. I suspect that now you question the wisdom and authority of these gods. If they are so powerful, why did they not attack themselves?"

"That was my thought, as well," mused Dour. "If their fear is so great, perhaps they no longer possess the power they once wielded. Perhaps now they are no stronger than the rest of the Duraden and cower in fear behind ancient traditions."

"It is truly a mystery," agreed Morthel. "A mystery I'm sure the admiral is busy unraveling as we speak."

"What do you mean?" asked Dour.

"As long as we all acted in good faith, our people would leave your sacred places untouched. However, with that act of treachery and aggression by the gods, the admiral will see them as enemies. By now that temple has been torn apart and anyone found inside, god or not, will face SUVI 5."

"That's not an enviable fate," sighed Ravel, as he leaned on his spear.

"No, it isn't," chuckled Morthel. "Let's go back to the ship and confer with the others, there's nothing of great interest here."

A Storm is Brewing

As EX2 rose above the city, Brodie's excited voice was heard. "Wait, I've got life signs, dozens of them, all Duraden."

"All stop."

"Ship is stopped, Captain."

"Now, let me see what's going on, Brodie." He stepped aside so she could reach the sensors. "You're right, there's quite a number of them. They seem to be milling around where we were, trying to figure out what we were up to, I expect. Three, take us up a little higher but stay over this area. I want to observe them a bit."

"Ship rising. Ship has stopped, Captain."

Thank you, Three," said Morthel as she stepped away from the sensors. "Brodie, put that up on the forward screen."

"Aye, Captain, forward screen."

The screen came alive with a view of a large number of Duraden milling around in the small courtyard where they had landed. Dressed in what looked like leather armor and carrying crude metal weapons, they were searching every nook and cranny. Two stood slightly apart, one directing the action while the other looked on. The lorespeaker stepped toward the screen and pointed. "There."

"Garanan?"

"Those two will be the lorespeaker and the chieftain."

"Lilly, on transporters, get a lock on those two. Thirteen, Connie, stunners at the ready."

"Aye, Captain," replied Connie as she passed the baby to Tommy, the medic. He stepped back and away from sight of the transport pad.

"Bring them up, Lilly."

"Transport engaged, Captain."

Even as she spoke, the two people arrived on the transport pad in a flash of light. Terrified, they shrank away from the people facing them.

The man raised his sword and Connie fired her stunner. He collapsed to the floor and lay twitching as Thirteen disarmed him.

Morthel stepped toward them, her posture relaxed, her hands visible and empty. "My name is Morthel, I'm captain of this ship. Make no aggressive moves and you will not be harmed." The box on her uniform repeated her words for the Duraden, but they didn't understand.

The older woman with the fancy headdress replied, but the language was different. Morthel waved her fingers to indicate she should speak further, but again, she didn't understand. Garanan stepped forward and, leaning on her staff, introduced herself. "I am Garanan, Lorespeaker of Bi-Lad Clan. We have travelled across the skies to seek out our kin in the forgotten lands."

Although she couldn't understand the words, this woman's regal bearing and manner suggested a response was required. She introduced herself, giving a number of titles and more. Thirteen had helped the chieftain back to his feet and returned the man's sword to the scabbard at his side. That man spoke as well, and the universal translator began to make sense of it.

Morthel tried again and, somewhat bemused at understanding a few words, the lorespeaker responded. A few tries later and the machine had the language. Both Duraden languages were basically the same root but had evolved differently.

"At last, we can now understand each other," said Morthel. "I'm Morthel, captain of this ship. Who are you?"

"I am Ordain, Lorespeaker of Argen Clan. My companion is Ornan, chieftain of the Argen. Where are we and how did we get here?"

"Friend Morthel, may I?"

"Go ahead, Garanan."

"I greet you, Ordain, I am Garanan of Bi-Lad Clan, Lorespeaker. We are now aboard Captain Morthel's magic ship, how she brought you here, I do not know."

"I know of many clans, but not the Bi-Lad. Have you traveled far?"

"Far indeed, Lorespeaker. Does your lore speak of three other lands, lands long forgotten?"

"Of course, but it has been untold generations since these lands were heard from. Are you indeed from a land far across the skies?"

"We are."

"Then you are the one the gods commanded us to kill." As he spoke, Ornan whipped out his sword, but Ravel's spear appeared at his throat. "You are one of our people, not of these others. Why would you defend them?"

"They are true friends," replied the youngster, then he grinned, "and extremely forgiving of young fools." He pulled back his spear.

"Put away your weapon, Chieftain," said Dour. "Ravel has just saved your life."

"This is getting way out of hand," said Morthel. "Remove your weapons now!" Wide-eyed they stared at her. When no one moved she spoke again. "Connie."

"Wait, wait," said Ordain. "Do as she says."

"Ordain?"

"They snatched us from the ground, felled you with magic, who knows what more they can do. Obey her, she obviously commands here." Reluctantly, he handed over his weapons. "We are your prisoners now. Contact our people, tell them of your demands. They will pay the ransom if they can."

"I want no ransom from you," sighed Morthel, "I merely want to talk with you. Sit here, listen to Garanan, we will show you the truth of what she says."

They sat where she indicated, then Garanan returned to the conversation. "Ordain, you say the gods commanded you to kill us, why did you not attack while we were on the ground?"

"To attack from hiding with greater numbers is unworthy and abhorrent to us, still the gods commanded it. They sounded frightened, and I hesitated to commit my people to a battle with people who could frighten the gods themselves."

"How did the gods contact you and when?" asked Morthel.

"Early this morning the voice spoke from the altar."

"How is it we can see your people below now, but earlier we could not?"

"I have no idea," replied Ordain, "perhaps it is because we were well beneath the ground, inside the ancient shelter."

"Perhaps," mused Morthel. "Tommy, see if you can contact the admiral for me."

"Aye, Captain."

"Now, Ordain, I ask you this, did the gods threaten to release a plague if you failed?"

"Yes."

"I have the admiral for you now, Captain."

Morthel stepped away and spoke to a voice from the air. "Admiral Sorenson."

"Here, Morthel. What's up?"

"Admiral, we've encountered a group of hostiles on Planet Two. For some reason they were undetected by our sensors until they reached the surface. We captured the two leaders, the chieftain and the lore speaker. They confessed the gods commanded them to kill us and they were threatened with the plague if they failed."

"Bring them to the Reacher. We'll await you in the briefing room."

"On our way, Admiral."

"You speak with your own gods; will they now make war on our gods?" asked Ornan.

"That voice belonged to our leader; you will soon meet her. Three, take us home."

"Returning to Reacher, aye."

Ravel chuckled. "Ornan, when you meet the admiral, be respectful."

Morthel smiled and brought up the three-dimensional display of the system. "Ornan, Ordain, this is a distant view of the four lands. Here is where we captured you, and over here is the homeland of Garanan, Dour, and Ravel. Here lie the other two ancient lands."

"Are there others of our people there as well?" asked Ordain.

"Probably, but we've not yet visited there. I'm quite certain we will before we leave this system. If you wish, I'll speak to the admiral and ask permission for you to accompany us, provided you give me assurances you will offer me or my people no threat."

Ordain sighed and looked Morthel in the eye. "You have spared our lives when it is clear you could have killed us easily. There will be no threat, Captain Morthel. If the gods want you dead, they will have to accomplish the task themselves."

Morthel chuckled at that. "Accepted."

"Approaching Reacher, Captain. We have landing clearance."

"Thank you, Three, take us home."

As they left the ship a security team was waiting to escort them to the briefing room. The room was full; all the captains, plus the passenger representatives, the Admiral, and Vice-Admiral were waiting for them. "Captain Morthel, please introduce your guests." The speaker was a woman, but the tightly controlled energy emanating from her sent waves of fear through Ornan and Ordain.

"Of course, Admiral. This woman is Ordain, lorespeaker of the Argen people, and this man is their chieftain, Ornan. People, this woman is Admiral Sorenson, our leader."

Jeannie stepped slowly toward them, trying to relax her posture. "Ordain, Ornan, on behalf of the people of the Wandering Fleet, I greet you. Answer my questions truthfully and I promise no harm will come to you."

"What's going to happen to us, will we ..."

Ordain put a gentle hand on his arm to silence Ornan. "We will answer your question truthfully, great Admiral. What would you know of us?"

"Thank you, Ordain. As I understand this, your gods commanded you to attack and kill our people."

"Yes."

"When did this happen?"

"At sunrise this morning," replied Ordain. "It is the custom to stand before the altar at sunrise, if the gods have any message for the people it will be delivered at this time. Often years pass without any contact, but this morning they came, they sounded fearful."

"Tell me, what was your reaction when they gave you this command?"

"Outrage," sighed Ornan, as he unbuckled the sword belt Morthel had returned to him, and let it drop to the floor. "All my life I have striven to live with honor, and this day I was commanded to cast that aside and strike from hiding at those who offered me no affront.

"When Ordain explained what would happen if we refused, we set about the task. The great bird commanded by Captain Morthel was already alighting and we hurried to the plaza where they would land. As promised, the gods hid our passage through the tunnels, but we arrived just as they were leaving.

"I was relieved, for the gods surely could not fault us for failing to kill an enemy we could not reach."

"And then we were snatched from the ground by Captain Morthel's magic," said Ordain.

The admiral began pacing about, her eyes glowing amber. This more than anything else, frightened the two Duraden. Finally, she stopped, resumed her seat, and returned her attention to the room.

"This is the second time your gods have commanded their people to kill us. If these gods are so all powerful, I wonder why they haven't made the attempt themselves. Opinions, people?"

Sheila Singh grinned as she spoke. "I'd say our little adventure that destroyed their defensive robots has them spooked. Who knows how many generations have utterly depended on that system? When we destroyed it, we probably sent them into a panic."

"Agreed, Sheila," sighed Jeannie, "but what exactly are we dealing with here?"

"Well, from here it looks like some of the old technology still functions," said Amanda. "Somebody still has access to it, perhaps a clan of the Duraden, or perhaps someone else. They've relied on the robots to keep the system isolated, and the tech to keep the Duraden subjugated."

"The thing to keep in mind here," said Rhonda, "is the threat they use, the possible plague. I'd like to call Carla and Dr. Reilley in for an opinion."

"Do it, Rhonda. I'd like to get their take on it myself."

Captain Rhonda Moore made the call, and within moments the two medics arrived. "What's up, Jeannie? Have you found something new and exciting in this system?"

"We may have, Eamon," smiled Jeannie. They'd had their issues in the past, but Eamon Reilley was the greatest medic in the fleet, that's why she'd made him Chief of Medical Research. "These folks are the Duraden. Their gods have threatened to release a plague against them if they don't manage to kill us."

"Okay, and you want us to find you an antidote, yes?"

"Yes, Eamon. First determine if there is a possible threat, and then give us an opinion of a possible antidote. Carla, if it comes to it, I'll need you to organize the mass inoculations, both for us and the Duraden."

The Chief of Medical for the fleet nodded, her mind already turning to the possibilities of mobilizing enough people to accomplish the task. "Carla, I'll need you to run tests on each and every one of us who have had any contact with the Duraden, and the Duraden themselves," said Dr. Reilley.

"Working," replied Carla, as she turned and left the room.

Eamon approached the Duraden. "Tell me about this plague."

"It's called the gray plague of death," replied Garanan.

"What does it look like? What does it do? What's the first sign of a person becoming sick?"

"At first a person becomes unable to perform simple tasks, for the body cannot remember the movements required. Within days the skin becomes gray and bleeds from the wrong places, then they slowly die. The process takes several days, they cannot eat, nor sleep, the teeth fall out . . . it is too horrible to contemplate."

"You've seen this yourself, haven't you?"

"Yes, when I was young. Of all my family, only I survived."

Eamon smiled at her as he spoke. "You may well become the one to save all your people from this plague forever."

Wide -eyed, Garanan stared at him for a long moment. "What do you mean?"

"If you withstood the disease, then something within your body managed to defeat it. My task will be to find that special something and create it on a grand scale. Carla's task will be to deliver it to every one of your people so the plague will never be able to affect them again.

"Tell me, did you bear children?"

"Yes, three, why do you ask?"

"I'll need to see them, to see if you passed the magic something on to them at birth."

She took a step back from him, but he held up his hands. "Be at peace, I won't harm you, nor will I harm your children. Work with me and see what happens. Once you're comfortable with the process, only then will I ask to meet the children."

Slowly, Garanan relaxed her fearful posture and nodded. "The great admiral has promised no harm will come to us. I will trust that and help you all I can."

"Then come, we'll go to the place where I work. Bring your guards if you wish." He left the room and she followed, leaving Dour and Ravel behind with Ordain and Ornan.

"All right, Amanda, recall any ships we might have out, and we'll all wait here for Eamon to bring us some answers. Rhonda, Sheila, keep your sensors tuned for any action on that god frequency of theirs. I want those gods found; they have much to answer for."

* * * * *

Back at the launch bay, Recovery One settled to the deck and the crew filed off. Brie was surprised to find Ebony waiting for her. "Commander Graves."

"Ebony, remember, just Ebony. So, any chances you've got time to sneak away with me for a treat at Simple Pleasures?"

"I'll make the time, and you know it," she grinned in reply.

A Waiting Game

Eamon Reilly led the lore speaker to his lab while the rest of them went with Carla to the medical bay. She demonstrated how she would get the samples from them by using one of her medics as a volunteer. The young man's grin as she took the readings put the Duraden at ease and they readily submitted to the tests.

Garanan was deep in conversation with Eamon when Carla delivered the samples. She smiled and set them on the table at his elbow. "Excuse me, Dr. Reilley, but I wonder, should we be quarantining people?"

"Too late for that now, Carla. Too many of our people have already been in contact with the Duraden and then mingled with the rest of us when they got home. We'll have to do this on a grand scale."

"I'll let engineering know to have more replicators built and ready." He chuckled as she walked away, then returned his attention to Garanan.

* * * * *

"Sorenson to Medical Research."

"Eamon here, Jeannie."

"It's been three days, Eamon, anything?"

"The damn thing is bacterial, our bio filters would easily detect it if it had made it aboard the ships, and it hasn't. Garanan does have a resistance to it in her system, the rest don't. I truly wish I had a live sample to study."

"And I'm glad you don't, remember the last time."

"Just don't shake the ship and it'll be fine, besides, you like SUVI 20."

He grinned at her chuckle. "Yes, I do. Eamon, any progress on a neutralizing agent to use against this thing? We need it for ourselves, but we need to set the Duraden free of it as well if we can."

"I'll need another day or two to be sure, and then we can start producing the serum. It'll take about a week to make enough."

"Do we have the necessary materials to create that much without depleting our supplies?"

"No worries, Jeannie. I asked Lilly Peters for samples of the grains she found, and the answer is there. It'll take a while to create, but we have all the material we need."

"Good to know, Eamon. As soon as possible, inoculate everyone in the fleet."

"Aye, Admiral."

* * * * *

Another week passed and they were ready, still another week to get everyone inoculated. Finally, all the SUVI were gathered with Eamon in a sealed room. "Eamon, no games now, tell me this won't awaken our dormant virus."

Dr. Eamon Reilly sighed and met the admiral's piercing gaze squarely. "Jeannie, ever since SUVI 20 walked out that door for the first time I've held nothing back from you, ever. You had every reason to maroon me with the rest of the criminals, but you gave me a chance to make up for what I've done.

"Standing right beside you is Tara, the woman I loved more than life itself, and the woman I risked my entire species for. She is now SUVI 20, and the closest thing I'll ever have to a daughter. I'd never risk harm to her, and you know it.

"The serum is safe to use on the SUVI, I tested it on a dormant virus before I told you it was ready."

"You did what? How???"

"On himself, Jeannie," said SUVI 20, as she stepped between them. "He was infected too, remember? If I know Eamon, and I do, he's taken dormant virus from his own blood to use for the test."

"Eamon?"

Again he sighed. "I was in an enclosed capsule with the antidote as well as a suicide drink with me in case I failed."

"An enclosed capsule? Where . . . the dead robot on Olga's ship, right? Olga and Moira helped you, didn't they?"

Eamon was carefully studying his shoes. "Yes. They prepped the bot, then did a site-to-site transport from the sealed lab, this one. Jeannie, please don't punish them, I ..."

She reached out to gently grip him by the shoulders. "I'm not going to punish anyone, Eamon, but I should have been kept in the loop here. You've got to stop this and consult with me before taking a chance like that."

"I didn't dare to, Jeannie," he said, bringing his gaze back to hers at last. "If I had, you'd have insisted on doing the test yourself, and we can't risk you, not like that. You're the one who keeps us alive against all odds, we need you; our collective species need you."

To his great surprise she said nothing, just gave his shoulders a gentle squeeze then released him and nodded. "I told you he was hopeless," grinned Twenty.

Jeannie chuckled and pushed up her sleeve. "Me first, then we wait; it shouldn't take long for the virus to react if it's going to." SUVI 18 stepped up with a tray of syringes. "Eighteen?"

"I've finished my training, Five. I'm now a full-fledged medic, specializing in SUVI medicine."

"Eighteen, I'm so proud of you I could split. What made you decide to be a medic?"

"It was Carla. When Thirteen got wounded and his virus went live, she gave direction, and I applied the bandages. She suggested we need a medic who is immune to the virus. We used Thirteen for a practice dummy for my first lesson."

"It went on for hours," groaned Thirteen, winking at Jeannie. "I looked like a walking mummy before they stopped."

Jeannie smiled at the playful banter between them; it was something new for the SUVI, something they could never have enjoyed in the caverns. "All right, Dr. Eighteen, how do you want us?"

"Just lineup here and I'll get you as you step past. There's no need to wait, it's all good."

"Okay," said Jeannie, "Dr. Eighteen says it's good, so let's get it done; then we have some gods to find and chastise."

* * * * *

Jeanie had already called Amanda and she'd arranged a full meeting of captains. Jeannie was pacing as usual. "All right everyone, we have to change our approach to this situation. I want fighter ships to make the first inspection of these planets, and each ship is to carry two extra medics with a large supply of serum just in case. Sheila, the Orca is too damn big for this, but you need to take up a central position so you can easily get to anyone in need of help."

"Understood, Admiral."

"Admiral, if I may."

"Morthel?"

"Admiral, my ship and crew are fully prepared to continue the first inspection, that's our job. I understand your concern but give me a couple more security people and I'll be fine." Jeannie gazed at the tiny, yet fierce, woman then relented.

"Yes, Morthel, it was your ancestors who built that extensive empire, and I don't doubt you, I don't. I have full faith in you, but please, be extra careful."

"I will, Admiral, after all, we have a baby on board."

Jeannie chuckled at that. "Hal, see she gets two of your best."

"On it, Admiral." With that he rose and left the room.

"All right, Morthel, you're going back to Planet Two. Investigate that altar and comb the rest of the planet for any indication at all of where we might find these gods. Sessas, you're going to Planet Three. Don't bother looking for salvage, just make sure it's clear for our explorers to explore."

"Sessas do."

"Hal, keep EX4 out in space and ready if anybody needs assistance and Sheila is otherwise occupied. F1 will go to Planet Four and scour it for the home of the gods. Linsey, Friendship will fly shotgun for Retriever. Twenty, I know that look, what's on your mind?"

"Well, Admiral, it seems to me the gods suddenly got concerned when we defeated the robots. Moira says she has the means to give the robots any command we want. What do you think, tow one back to where it can function and command it to lead us to Olympus. That was the home of the gods to an old Earth ..."

"I know what Olympus was. I've warned you before about teasing me. Sessas, get her out of here and put her to work."

There was the sound of Sessas' hissing laughter. "Aye, Admiral. Tentee, come. We go Planet Three, stir up trouble. You bring Warhammer just in case." Everyone was chuckling as they left.

"Okay, the troublemakers are on the way, Olga, talk to Moira about Twenty's idea. If she thinks it'll work, take your ships out that way and stand by."

"Aye, Admiral."

"Meeting adjourned, people. Sorenson to SUVI 9."

"Here, Five."

"Warm up the ship, we're going out."

"Aye, Admiral, warming up. Is the Vice-Admiral to accompany us?"

"No."

"Yes," said Amanda.

Jeannie arched an eyebrow at Amanda who gave her a determined look. "It seems I've been overruled, Nine. The Vice-Admiral will be joining us."

"Understood," came the chuckling response.

"Mandy."

"No, Jeannie. If you leave me here, I'll be bored to tears, nothing to do except watch Rhonda and Maxi gaze into each other's eyes and get all gooey."

"That's it," declared Rhonda, blushing, "I have a ship to run. You guys go start a fight or something and let me work."

"Aye, aye, Captain," grinned Jeannie, as she and Amanda linked arms and left.

Return to Planet Two

During the time spent waiting on Reacher, SUVI 13 and Dour had spent hours trading stories of successful hunts. Ornan and Connie had engaged in Connie's hobby, fencing. The swords were much lighter than he was used to, but he caught on fast.

The two lore speakers spent most of their waking hours with Linsey, teaching her their language as she wanted to learn it without the translator units. There was a lot of laughter at her first attempts. Her problem was that the original language had evolved differently on each planet.

The most unusual friendship to grow out of the situation was Ravel and Brodie. For some strange reason the two young men bonded. Ravel had a keen interest in learning about the technology, and battered Brodie with questions. Brodie just chuckled as he took the time to explain the basics of what he did and why, enjoying the role of teacher.

Ravel also had a sense of how Brodie would succumb to frustration, and asked questions in a way that forced the young engineer to slow down and explain. That process often brought about the solution to the problem. As their friendship grew, they became almost inseparable.

When all was finally ready, they set out. As EX2 approached the planet, Connie was handing out weapons. "I'm sorry, Commander Peters, but for this part of the mission I need to commandeer your crew for extra security."

"Understood, Connie. How do you want to do this?"

"Your crew will hold back to secure the ship, leaving the three of us free to accompany Thirteen as he hunts up some trouble to get into."

"Works for me. Captain?"

"I like it, Lilly, Connie. Thirteen, this is no longer an explore mission, it's a hunt for a hostile entity, location and attributes unknown. You'll lead the ground search and I'll work from the ship. We'll stay in close contact by comms."

"Aye, captain. Where would you like to start?"

"Let's start with Ornan's people. Ordain, Ornan, I ask you now, will you help or hinder us?"

They looked at each other and then faced Morthel. "We will help you, Captain Morthel," replied Ordain. "It is clear your people could easily have killed us and all our people. Our unseen gods fear you and threatened us, yet had not the courage to face you themselves. We will help you all we can. What must we do?"

"First, lead Thirteen to the passages that hid your approach from us, then take us to the altar where the gods contact you."

"I'd like to have an engineer with me, Captain," said Thirteen, "someone with a better understanding of possible technology than I have. Three could come with us."

"I'll go," said Brodie. Thirteen turned to grin at him. "You're going into the tunnels, right? I'll be fine."

"Accepted. Captain?"

"Are you sure, Brodie?" asked Morthel.

"I have to beat this thing, Captain. I've got to be able to function."

"I'll go with him, Captain Morthel," said Ravel. "I'll take my spear and, if necessary, thump him on the head with it until he comes to his senses."

"My buddy Ravel, always ready to help me out," groaned Brodie.

"All right, Brodie, you and your personal physician are with Thirteen. Where are we, Three?"

"Directly above the courtyard where we found our guests."

"Well done. Shields. Set us down, Three."

"Ship has landed, Captain."

"Thank you, Three. Ordain, Ornan, now we come to it."

"How can we best assist you, Captain Morthel?" replied Ornan. "Our gods have proven themselves unworthy, threatening us with disease and worse, but your people have helped us and found a way to defeat the plague. What do you need us to do?"

"Go to your people, Ornan, and tell them of all that has happened. Tell them not to interfere with us and they will not be harmed. Ordain, take us to the altar where the gods speak to you.

"Connie, you, Thirteen, and your forces; secure the area. Lilly, arm your people and prepare to hold the ship. Brodie, Ravel, you're with me."

Dour stepped forward. "With permission, Captain Morthel, I will hunt with my brother, Thirteen."

"Granted. Connie, go."

The hatch swung open and a hail of arrows and spears struck the shields. "Stop, stop," shouted Ornan as he leaped from the ship. "Stop or they'll kill you all!"

"Ornan? Is that you, Chieftain?" asked a tall Duraden as he stepped from hiding. "Is the Lorespeaker with you?"

"I am here, Ethran, as you can see," said Ordain, as she stepped from the ship. "Lower all your weapons and these people won't harm you."

"We're not afraid, Ordain, and the gods have chosen a new Lorespeaker."

"The gods are false, and ..."

"Enough of this," said Morthel, as she stepped from the ship. "Lilly, drop the shields, Connie, secure the area."

"On stun," shouted Connie, as she charged forward. The battle was swift and predictable. Blades and blunt instruments bounced off the advanced armor, and the speed of the coordinated attack stunned the Duraden. Within moments they were down, disarmed, and in restraints.

"Lilly, detail two to watch them. Ordain, lead on."

"This way," she replied, as she led them into a building and down a flight of stairs.

As they went, Brodie was busy taking readings with a hand-held instrument. "It looks like this passageway was lined with some sort of shielding, Captain."

"Understood, Brodie, keep checking."

After a long series of turns they arrived at the altar room. A number of Duraden were there to defend the doors, but they were no match for the weapons that faced them. Ordain opened the doors then stood aside to let Morthel enter.

"Who enters the sacred hall?" demanded a voice from the ether.

"I do. I'm Morthel of Reacher, Earalith species. Identify yourselves." Only silence greeted her. She gave it a few moments then spoke again. "I'm one of those you wanted killed. I hold no such aspirations about you. Come out of hiding and speak with me as equals."

"Equals? You are not our equal, we are gods, you are mortal."

"You're strange gods who would threaten to destroy your own people if they fail to do what you dare not attempt. It appears to me that you believe the Duraden to be more powerful than you."

"Blasphemy!" shouted the voice. "Kill them, kill them now."

Grinning with delight, Morthel turned to Brodie. "Anything?"

"They're broadcasting all right, Captain. I believe it isn't hard-wired, but wireless. If you can keep them at it long enough Reacher is sure to track the signal."

"Good work Brodie." Morthel turned back to the altar. "Tell me, gods of the Duraden, why do you fear us so? We have offered no harm to you or your people. Why command our deaths?"

"You're an abomination," roared the voice. "You must be eradicated."

The voice continued to rant, but Morthel's attention was elsewhere. Brodie was signaling her excitedly. "In there, Captain, it's in there behind that slab of stone." He was clearly terrified.

"Easy, Brodie. Tell me what's in there?"

He swallowed hard and took a deep breath as Ravel laid a calming hand on his shoulder. "A gas canister, Captain. A really big canister. Could be the plague gas."

"All right, Brodie, calm yourself, we've all been inoculated against the plague, but I get your point. Thirteen, see if you can move the slab. Brodie see if you can disarm any triggering mechanism that might be there. Isolate the damned thing."

The rant had stopped so she turned back to the altar, motioning Ordain to join her."

"Here is your Lorespeaker," she said. "See how small I am beside her? She has no fear of me, so why do you?"

"You are an abomination. You must be eradicated."

"Oh come on, seriously? See how unafraid Ordain is? She knows we won't harm her or her people. Come out of hiding and talk to us. We can share information so all can benefit."

"Noooooo! You will all die a horrible death."

Try as she might, Morthel got no further response from the altar. Something behind her began to spark and crackle, but suddenly stopped as Brodie brought his boot down hard on it. He was pale and sweating, trembling with the effort to hold himself together. "I believe my friend was successful, Captain Morthel," chuckled Ravel.

"Well done, Brodie." Morthel reached for her comm. "Morthel to EX2."

"Lilly here, Captain."

"How are things going up there?"

"Our guests are all awake, Captain, but they're being quiet. Twenty-One's SUVI sensors say we're all good here."

"Excellent. Can the sensors find us down here? Will the transporter reach us?"

A moment passed then she got her answer. "We have you on sensors, Captain, and the transporters will reach easily."

"Bring Ordain and me home, Lilly. Thirteen see what else you can hunt up here then return to the ship."

"Aye, Captain." She and Ordain vanished in a flash of light; Thirteen turned to Brodie. "Well done, you disarmed the gas canister;

now let's see if we can find anything else that will lead us to the prey." There was a different look in his eye and Brodie swallowed hard. He wouldn't want this man on his trail.

A close inspection of the altar found the receiver and speakers as well as a video camera, but little else. "That's it, Thirteen," sighed Brodie. "I've got their frequency, but nothing more."

At that point Connie's comm pinged. "Here, Captain."

"You've got incoming, Connie, about thirty signals moving in a tight formation. We can pull you out."

"Negative, Captain, Thirteen wants to talk to them."

"All right. Connie, take no chances and no prisoners. I'm getting tired of this."

"Understood, Captain. Brodie, you and Ravel behind the altar. We'll defend the door."

A few moments later, a troop of Duraden arrived in tight formation. Two leaped through the door brandishing energy weapons and shouting. "We are the Kurk, chosen of the gods to wield the god weapons." A heartbeat later they were face down on the floor, unarmed, and Thirteen was standing over them.

A hail of weapons fire came through the doorway, but the only casualties were the two Thirteen had disarmed. He had taken cover with Brodie and Ravel. "Touchy bunch of buggers," he grinned. "What do you think of their weapons, Brodie?"

"What???"

"Their weapons, what are they, what are their capabilities?"

"How the hell should I know?"

"Here's one I took off them. Dismantle it and see what you can learn."

Three more made it through the door but were cut down by Connie and her small force. Ravel reached out to touch Thirteen on the arm. "Challenge their leader to single combat, he dares not refuse. Challenge him for leadership of them all."

"What do you mean?"

"Ornan told us about the Kurk. It's their way, the strongest leads, the rest obey. With those god weapons they will enslave all of Ornan's people. If you defeat him, you can command them to destroy the weapons."

Thirteen sighed, this was something he understood. He looked to Dour who nodded. "I challenge the leader of the Kurk," he bellowed as he stood up. "Come out and face me, stop hiding behind walls and sending others to do the work you're afraid to do."

A deep voice responded to his taunt. "You need two of the true people to stand as seconds, Alien. Who will stand for you?"

"I am Dour-den of Bi-Lad Clan, I will stand for my brother hunter."

"As will I. I am Ravel of Bi-Lad Clan."

"I've never heard of Bi-Lad Clan."

"We come from a far-off land," replied Dour. "One of the four lands of legend."

"I don't believe you."

"Come out from hiding and see for yourself."

The hidden man knew he could not refuse, and reluctantly, led two more into the altar room. The two Duraden stood beside Thirteen and he could not deny they were of his own species. "I repeat the challenge," said Thirteen. "Single combat for the leadership."

"This is a fight to the death, are you prepared to die, Alien?"

"I am."

Without warning the Duraden leaped at Thirteen, a long blade flashing toward his throat. He missed as Thirteen easily ducked the blow and moved behind him. Powerful arms encircled the man's throat. He was ripped from his feet then tossed to the floor, twitching, his neck broken.

A moment later the body was still and Thirteen spoke. "But not today. I have defeated your leader. Come forward and lay down your weapons or challenge me, one or the other." One by one they came, tossing aside their weapons.

"Are there any more of these weapons?"

"No, leader, these are all."

"Some of you remain here to deal with the bodies of your dead, the rest of you take me to the place where the weapons were stored."

The one he spoke to motioned to the others. Several began to carefully arrange the dead then carry them away. Meanwhile Thirteen and his retinue were led through a long corridor to another door. Through that door was an arsenal with one empty crate. "All your weapons came from this crate?"

"Yes, Leader."

"Do you know the function of these things?"

"No, Leader. The gods directed us to the red crate and gave us instruction on how to make the weapon function. Leader, may I ask a question?"

"Go ahead."

"What are you? You are not of our people."

"I'm SUVI. Long ago on a faraway land a plague came to my people, only nineteen of us survived. I was the thirteenth survivor, and that is my name now, Thirteen. I was once human like these people, but no longer." The man nodded as Thirteen turned away and reached for his comm.

"Thirteen to EX2."

"EX2 here. Report."

"We've settled our differences with the Kurk, and the survivors have shown us to an arsenal. There's too much here for EX2 to carry. You might want to send for the Recovery ships."

"Understood. Do you want a transport out?"

"Negative, Captain. We'll remain here to guard the cache until further orders, then we'll resume the hunt."

"Acknowledged. Stand by. EX2 out."

* * * * *

"What is it, Captain?"

"It seems that Thirteen has found a cache of weapons and wants the salvage ships to come and pick them up. I'll check in with Reacher and see what I can do. EX2 calling Reacher."

"Rhonda here, Morthel, what do you need?"

"SUVI 13 has located an arsenal of modern weapons and says there's too many for us to carry. Any chance Olga might come down for a look?"

"I'll check and let you know. Reacher out." A few short moments later she was back. "Reacher to EX2."

"Here, Rhonda."

"Recovery One and Two are on their way. Harlan and Jake are with them."

"Tell them to contact Thirteen, he's a long way from home right now."

"Understood. Reacher out."

"EX2 to Thirteen."

"Here, Captain."

"Both salvage ships plus Jake and Harlan are on their way. They'll contact you for coordinates to the cache."

"Understood."

* * * * *

"I wonder what this one does," mused Ravel, as he picked up a strange object. "It looks like a spear."

Brodie's hand appeared on his and pressed down. "Put it down, carefully."

"Does it bite?"

"If it does, we could all be sorry, or dead."

"All right then," said Ravel, as he lowered the weapon and released his grip on it. "I bow to your superior wisdom." He was grinning and Brodie sighed as he rolled his eyes.

The Kurk all backed away fearfully as armed people suddenly appeared in the room. "Wow, Thirteen, looks like you found the treasure."

"I did, Jake, but this is getting out of hand. This needs to be removed or destroyed."

"Agreed. We've got this if you want to get on with the hunt."

"You know me too well," chuckled Thirteen. He turned to the men who had led him to this place.

"Kurk, hear me. You are the strongest and most able of the Duraden. I challenge you now to use your strength and cunning to help and defend the rest of your people, to keep them safe and happy. This is the way to prove yourselves worthy. Do you have the courage to take up that challenge?"

"Is that the way of your people, Leader?" asked one man, as he stepped forward.

"Yes, it is the way of the SUVI," said Jake. "They are few, but they are mighty and well respected."

The man turned to the others and slowly they nodded their agreement. "Then it will be the way of the Kurk as well."

"Good," said Thirteen. "Now, show me the place where food is placed for the gods."

"This way, Leader." It was only a short walk to another door which the man opened. Inside was a large dais, nothing more. "This is the place. The kill is placed there and the next day it's gone."

"Brodie?"

The young man glanced at his instrument again then sighed. "Only a transport pad, nothing more."

"Is there any way to get the coordinates of the destination from it?"

"I can't detect any other technology here. Just what's needed to run the pad."

"Run the pad?"

"Yes, in case someone wanted to transport in, they'd need the beacon. All these buildings are shielded for some reason."

"Damn, looks like we'll have to do this the hard way. Thirteen to Captain Morthel."

"Morthel here."

"The salvage crews have arrived and have this area well in hand. Captain, I have an idea of how we can track down these elusive gods, but we'll need the help of the Reacher, and the rest of the fleet needs to be informed and ready."

"What's the plan?"

"The Duraden hunt and gather to survive, and they make sacrifices of food to the gods. They place the food on a transport pad then it disappears in the night. My guess is the gods are monitoring the pad and wait until the hunters leave before they transport it out.

"I want to go hunting, then put a tracker on the kill and leave it on the pad for the gods to enjoy. If the whole fleet is tuned in to the frequency of the tracker, someone should be able to pick up the signal from the destination."

"Thirteen, my friend, you never disappoint. I love it. You go and I'll alert the fleet. Morthel out."

"All right, Kurk, let's go hunting," grinned Thirteen. "Brodie, transport back to EX2 and get a tracker ready, make sure the rest of the fleet has the frequency."

"On it, boss," sighed Brodie, as Ravel slapped him on the shoulder then trotted off after the hunting party.

A Wide Net

"Well, it's a bust," sighed Billy, as he lowered his weapon. "Twenty?"

"Looks like it," she agreed. "SUVI 20 to Retriever."

"Sessas, here."

"We've come up empty again, Captain. We captured the altar without killing anyone, but the gods won't talk to us. What's next?"

"Come home, we make new plan."

"On our way, Captain. Okay guys, let's go."

While SUVI 20 led the strikers back to the ship, Captain Sessas sat lost in thought. This one truly was a puzzle. Just as on the other two planets, Planet Three turned up two groups of Duraden living as hunter/gathers. All had been instructed to kill the newcomers, all failed, then led their captors to the altars. Nothing more was found, and the gods would no longer respond to the newcomers.

"Anything?" asked SUVI 20, as she arrived back at the ship.

"Signal scattered, not able to track," replied Sessas.

"Crap. Paranoid buggers."

"Assholes."

"You got that right, my sister. What's our next move?"

"Big planet, keep looking."

"Works for me," sighed Twenty, as she settled into a seat. The fighter ship rose easily into the air and continued their search.

* * * * *

"That's the third batch, Five," said SUVI 9, as he gathered the weapons from the fallen Duraden. "The altar can't be far away."

"Agreed. Keep an eye on Amanda while she makes friends with these folks. I want to go poke around a bit."

"Understood."

Amanda Drake came out of the ship to find SUVI 9 and crew waiting for her. "Let me guess, you're my bodyguards; she's gone hunting."

"Your insights serve you well, Vice-Admiral," chuckled SUVI 9. "Shall I wake up some of these folks for you?"

"Please do, Nine. Let's see if we can have any better luck with this lot."

They didn't, and at the end of the day all ships but EX2 returned to Reacher.

On the Hunt

Ensign Brie Elliot sighed as she stepped down from the ship and into the landing bay. She looked all around, but that which she wanted to see wasn't there. "Ah well, she's probably busy as usual. Trying to get Ebony to relax for a few minutes is a real challenge, the girl never stops." Suddenly the comm on her uniform pinged.

"Brie here."

"Ensign Elliot, report to VR studio one."

"Acknowledged." Puzzled, she set out for the passenger area of the great ship. She looked sadly at the line-up waiting to get into Simple Pleasures and wondered why she was being called to the VR studio. Perhaps they were working on a med program.

"Ah, our guest of honor at last," said a tall young man in a Simple Pleasures apron. "Right this way, Ensign Elliot." He seated her at a table that was set up like one in the café. "Commander Graves will join you shortly. Earalithian tea and cake?"

"Huh? Oh, yes please."

He hurried away then soon returned with cake and tea for two. Ebony was close behind him. "Hi, like my little surprise?"

"Ebony, this is awesome, but I don't understand."

"We're always getting hustled out of the café; I came up with this so we can take our time and enjoy."

"You pulled in favors so you would have more time with me?"

"Yup."

"Wow. I'm flattered, but I get the sense you're up to something."

"Brie, I'm shocked that you doubt my sincerity."

"Okay, now I know you're up to something."

"She's got you there, Ebony."

"Hush, Edran, you're not helping."

Edran giggled and returned to their computer station. Ebony grinned as Brie shook a finger at her. "All right, I'll talk. First, I did set this table situation up for us so we could have more time together, and it's a permanent fixture. We now have a direct line into the café.

"Second, we need to make a training VR for the medics on the small ships. This isn't a train-from-scratch medical training VR, it's to take a fully trained medic and make them ready for work on a small ship. I was hoping to talk you into volunteering to help us."

Brie was smiling shyly now, knowing full well that Ebony had been finding ways for them to have more time together. "Okay, what would I have to do?"

"Put up with me following you around for days, taking video of you doing what you do at work."

"I think I could manage that." She smiled and reached for Ebony's hand. "I can see the trouble you've gone to, trying to find us more free time together, and I want you to know I appreciate it."

"But?"

"No buts, Ebony, not a single one, just promise me something."

"Anything at all, sweet woman."

"Oh, now that has potential."

Ebony laughed and blushed deeply. "Stop it, you nut. What was it you wanted?"

"Just promise to stay out of the pilot's seat."

* * * * *

While Ebony and Brie were enjoying a few stolen moments, Thirteen was hunting. The Kurk guided him up to the surface, and then they set out to find prey. Darkness fell and they wanted to retreat below to the underground tunnels for the night, but he refused. Thirteen was a lot happier out in the open, with Brodie back on the ship he no longer had to stay underground.

The Kurk were nervous above ground at night, but the leader stayed, so they stayed. He appeared to be sleeping soundly, but each time one of them looked his way he opened his eyes. This man was accustomed to hunting alone, and although he rested, he slept lightly. Dawn found him ready for the hunt.

The sun was just reaching the broken streets when they spotted a small group of tall, big-bodied creatures feasting on some wild grain. They were extremely watchful, and the hunters were well out of reach. Thirteen grinned and motioned for Dour to join him. "What do you think; can you reach them with a spear?"

"Perhaps you could make that kill from this distance, but not I. I could reach them, but not with a killing throw, probably not even wound one. I'd want to be much closer."

"Ever hunt with just a knife?"

"Never, have you?"

"Far too many times. As a slave I wasn't trusted with many weapons and the hunt was usually with a knife or spear if I could make and hide one for future use. I rarely get to hunt anymore so everybody stay here; I'll make the kill." He slipped a long-bladed knife into each hand and faded into the shadows.

They watched as he slowly worked his way toward the prey. The sun rose higher and higher, yet he was barely halfway to his target. Suddenly one of the beasts swept its head up, looking away from Thirteen. He rose from the broken rubble and threw one knife with tremendous force. The weapon buried itself in the animal's body and it stumbled then fell to the ground.

A roar came from the side away from Thirteen, and a huge cat-like creature charged toward the downed animal, so did he. Moving at a speed that equaled that of the predator and astonished the watching Duraden, he arrived at the kill at the same time as the beast.

The predator leaped at him, but Thirteen met the charge and leaped away. The beast turned to face him, bleeding profusely from a gaping wound in its side. Thirteen balanced lightly on the balls of his feet as he prepared for the creature to charge again. It came at him, claws raking and fangs reaching for him, but again it missed and took another deep wound.

The animal turned and crouched but was pierced by several spears and it relaxed on the ground as the life force left it. The Duraden stood well back from Thirteen, gazing at him in wonder and somewhat fearfully. He was inspecting one shoulder where a claw had ripped away his armor, his remaining weapon dripped blood from the blade, and his eyes were a deep amber.

Finally he nodded. "Kurk, prepare the kill. We will take it to the place of sacrifice." With that, he reached for his comms and called. "Thirteen to EX2."

"EX2 here, Thirteen. How goes the hunt?"

"Successful, Captain. Does Brodie have a tracker ready for us?"

"He does. Just a moment."

Brodie suddenly appeared in the space beside Thirteen. He swallowed hard but didn't panic. "Which one?"

"That one," replied Thirteen. "Hide it well, Brodie, but make sure it's working."

Brodie nodded, and keeping his eyes on the kill, knelt and embedded the device in the meat. He then checked his instruments. "Done. It's working. Brodie to EX2."

"EX2 here, Brodie. Receiving that signal loud and clear. Prepare for return transport." A moment later he disappeared.

"All right," said Thirteen, "let's get this beast on the sacrifice pad." The Kurk led the way back, some of them carrying the dead animal. They were in awe of the man who had become their leader. Once the offering was in place, Thirteen called for transport back to the ship.

The Kurk silently returned to their homes to take up the challenge he had given them.

* * * * *

Amanda Drake had transported back to Reacher where she was coordinating the fleet. Each of the four planets had two ships monitoring, listening for the signal from Thirteen's tracker. Deep in the night, the offering vanished from the transport pad and the tracker sent out a clear signal.

An Elusive Prey

"Got the signal. That's us, we're the closest," shouted Kumar, First Officer of the Retriever. "Suit up, Strikers."

Captain Sessas was out of her sleeping cabin before he finished speaking. "Where?"

"Below us and about two hundred kilometers ahead, in those mountains, Captain. Ship is already closing."

"Is good. Strikers ready?"

"Ready, Captain," replied Billy, as the strike force gathered at the hatch.

"Shields!"

"Are we there yet?" yawned SUVI 20, as she exited her booth.

"Almost," grinned the pilot.

"Guns or armor, Captain Sessas?" asked Twenty.

"Armor."

"Looks like I'm with you guys, Billy," she grinned as she pulled on her armor.

"Me too," said Sessas, as she gathered her own armor. "Kumar, you have ship, land us close. Billy, Rayla, Connor, you team one, Sessas and Tentee team two."

"Understood, Captain."

Suddenly the small ship shook slightly under the impact of weapons fire, but the shields held easily. "Guns!"

"Aye, Captain," came the reply as the gunner opened fire.

"Evade!"

"Evading, aye."

"How many?"

"Three left, make that two," replied SUVI 20. "Down to one. And we're clear."

"What hit us?"

"Robots, Captain, five in all," replied the man on sensors. "They came up from that open hangar ahead, our original target."

"Kumar, get us down."

"Ship has landed, Captain."

"Go!" The hatch flew open and the strike force leaped out, Twenty and Sessas going right and the other three to the left. At Sessas' nod, Rayla leaped inside and dove for cover, followed by Billy and Connor. Twenty and Sessas followed.

Ahead lay a short corridor, then a closed door. SUVI 20 struck the door like a hurricane, her war hammer leading the way. The door was blasted from the hinges and flew inward. Sessas led the strikers through, but the place was empty.

Calls of "Clear!" echoed as the strikers swept through, checking every nook and cranny, every room. It took a while and just as they finished SUVI 5 and her crew came pouring through the doorway.

"Is empty, Admiral," said Sessas. "We find signal, come. Attacked by robots, destroy, but assholes escape while we fight."

"Understood, Sessas. They got away, but it's not your fault. I'll call the salvage crews down to empty this place out. We'll find them, don't worry."

Sessas nodded. "Why bother? Gods no real threat."

"Not to us."

"But to Duraden folk. Sessas understand."

* * * * *

The fleet captains met with the admiral in the briefing room of the Reacher. "Everybody's here, Admiral."

"Thank you, Vice-Admiral Drake. All right, people, it's time to see where we stand. Olga, how's the salvage going?"

"We've been busy, Admiral. The cargo bay is running out of room so we're switching over to harvesting those grain fields. The botanists say it's rich in nutrients, a real find."

"Excellent. Rhonda."

"On the home front, this system is a real treasure trove, new and useful metals, some tech improvements, and a super new food source. Nobody's shooting at us anymore and I'm happy."

Jeannie chuckled at that. "Looks like the home ship is in good shape. Sessas."

"Assholes send robots, we defeat, but assholes escape. Ship good, no damage, crew good, no injuries."

"And therein lies the problem, people. The prey is elusive for certain. We investigated that nest of them Sessas found, but they were gone. Sadly, that wasn't a home base, merely an outpost, in use for generations, but no signs that there were any permanent residents."

"How can you tell, Jeannie?" asked Captain Baris, the admiral's grandfather.

"The place was cleaned out, Grandfather, nothing left behind. There were no large food storage areas as would be needed for families, no large food prep stations, nothing for children or elders, no medical station. No, this was just a military outpost.

"The big question is where did they go? There was no escape tunnel, so they transported out, but to where?"

"Planet One," sighed Ka'Ron, as he laid aside the tablet he had glanced at. "Our sensors managed to pick up the beam and log it but didn't flag it. Our ever-curious Maccay discovered it in one of their routine reviews of general scans. I've just now been informed."

"Gone to ground again," sighed Jeannie, as she sank back into her chair. "Grandfather, Olga, Sheila, you three were trained in classic military style on old Earth. Speculate, what are we dealing with here and how do we root them out?"

"Well," said Captain Baris, "I'd say this system was conquered by an outside force. The victors left a system in place to keep the Duraden from ever advancing to threat status again, and to prevent any other explorers from coming in contact with them. They apparently left a small force in place to make sure that system worked.

"The question now is, are these just military outposts? If so they must be serviced, and troops replaced from another system. However, I doubt that is the case."

"Why?"

"They force the Duraden to provide them with food. If they were being dropped in from afar, they would most likely bring their own rations, or hunt for their own food. No, I expect that somewhere in this system we'll find a colony of them."

"Olga, Sheila, do you agree with his assessment?"

"Oh yes," replied Olga Volkov. "Frank's right, besides, it's been a long time since the Duraden were defeated; whatever species did this is probably long gone by now. We haven't found a single piece of tech or metals that look recent. Everything appears to be centuries old."

"Sheila?"

"I agree, it's the only thing that makes sense."

Jeannie stood and started pacing. "Then why the hell can't we find them?" Suddenly she stopped. "The caverns. We can't find them because they're underground, and on Planet One I'm willing to bet."

"What makes you say that, Jeannie?"

"Because they're the prey now and they know it, Grandfather. We nearly got some of them and they fled."

"Back to their lair," he grinned.

"Precisely. Morthel, you explored that whole planet?"

"We did, Admiral. We found nothing that would indicate a colony of space farers."

"Maybe you did. Can you get me a 3-D map of planet One?"

"Of course, Admiral. I have everything we got from that planet right here." She laid her tablet on the long table, touched a few buttons, then a holographic map of Planet One appeared over the long table.

"Show me every place you found evidence of the Duraden." Blue dots suddenly glowed on the map. "These are all Duraden?"

"Yes, Admiral. Once we had made friends with Garanan's people we didn't stop to chat with the other clans."

"Hmm, they all seem to be here in the northern continent and this smaller one to the south. This area over here showed no signs of life?"

"No, Admiral, this western continent is quite mountainous, and we found no signs of intelligent life there."

"Yes, and the mountains would be a likely place to find deep caverns, or to create them. Morthel, Sessas, reconfigure your sensors to probe deeper into the ground. Go over every inch of that continent, find me those elusive gods.

"Hal, prep EX4, you and I will fly shotgun for them."

"You won't mind if I tag along, will you, Admiral?"

"Was I forgetting to take our warship when I go to battle, Sheila?"

Sheila matched her grin. "You gave me all the best toys."

"All right but keep an eye out behind as well. I don't want anything sneaking up on us either."

"I will, Admiral. Probie is also flying rear guard. If anything new shows up she'll let us know before it gets too close."

"Then let the hunt begin. Meeting adjourned."

* * * * *

"All EX4 personnel to the ship on the double."

"Aw crap," sighed Ebony. "Ah well, duty calls." She leaped to her feet, kissed Brie on the cheek then fled the studio.

Brie just shook her head and chuckled. "And there she goes. Hey, Edran, you want the rest of her cake?"

"Yes I do." Edran sat in the chair Ebony had just vacated and devoured the cake. "That is so good."

"Yes it is, my friend."

"Ebony really likes you."

"I really like her, Edran, but I think she likes flying a ship more than she likes me."

"Nope."

"Nope? Why do you say nope?"

"Because she moved that medic VR way up on the list. It was a really low priority."

"Really? So, what would you say are my chances here?"

"Better than average," grinned Edran, as they headed back to the computer station.

"I'll take it," said Brie, as she followed Edran over. "How could I up my game, do you think?"

"You're a medic, you help hurt people. Ebony helps hurt people too. Maybe there's a way for you to work together on one of her projects."

"Her projects?"

"Ebony always has some scheme or other going on that will help people find fun things to do."

"Like you?"

"Yeah, like she did with me. Now I get to do fun stuff every day and even the admiral says it's important."

"It is important, Edran. She did the same for Alli too, didn't she?"

"Yes. Now all you need to do is think of a project for her and help her with it. That should level up your chances."

Edran was giggling as Brie shook a finger at them and walked away. "Level up my chances eh? Why not, could be fun at that. Now, what kind of a project could I come up with? Hmmm."

* * * * *

"Is the ship ready?" asked Morthel, as she returned to EX2.

"Ship is ready, passengers and crew are aboard, Captain," replied Lilly. "Sensors configured for deep probe."

"Three, take us back to Planet One."

"Planet One, aye. Launching now." The ship rose and slipped out of Reacher's cargo bay to streak toward the planet.

"Here are the coordinates for the search."

"Thank you, Captain. Logging now."

* * * * *

For two days, both ships combed that mountain range, crossing and crisscrossing each other's search patterns, all to no avail. At length they gave up and returned to the Reacher where the admiral called a full meeting of the captains.

"All right, people, let's have it. Rhonda, report."

"Reacher is all topped up, Admiral, the storage areas are full to bursting, all hydroponics are busy developing new food sources, incorporating the new grains Commander Peters brought us. The salvage bays are jammed so full of salvage it's hard to get around down there. If this system has anything more for us, I don't know where we'd put it.

"The ship herself is fit as a fiddle and ready to go."

"Good to know. Sheila?"

"Orca is also in top form, Admiral. We've even got the overflow of salvage in our fighter bay."

"Excellent."

"Olga?"

"Both ships are in perfect working order, Admiral, however, we had to stop bringing in salvage and grain; there was nowhere to put it."

"So now we come to it, it's down to the fighters and explorers. Morthel?"

"Well, Admiral, from an exploratory point of view, we've been all over Planet One and Planet Two and found much the same thing. I doubt we'll find anything different on Planet Three or Four."

"We didn't," sighed Jeannie.

"From the search-for-the-gods angle, we've come up empty," said Morthel. "I really thought Thirteen's tracker would yield us better results, but the enemy seems to have vanished into the mountains.

Sessas and I combed that area for two days, checking and double checking each other's results, but nothing. Not one sign of them."

"And that's what has me flummoxed," grumbled Jeannie. "By every instinct I have, they should be there."

"I agree, Admiral," said SUVI 20. "Every sense I have tells me they're in there, somewhere."

"Do we care?" asked Captain Baris. "We have everything we could gather from this system. We could just move on."

"If we do, the Duraden will pay the price for it," said Linsey da Silva.

Suddenly Morthel's info pad buzzed softly. She glanced at it, then reached for her comm. "Say again, Brodie, the others will want to hear this."

"Captain Morthel, I've been going over the sensor logs and noticed something, an odd reading we got in two places. The first time was on Planet Two when we didn't see the Duraden until they came above ground, the second time was in an area of the mountains we were searching. Captain, I believe we can't find them because they have something to fool up our sensors."

"Dammit, that's it," declared Jeannie, as she banged her fist on the table. "Well done, Brodie, well done. Can you identify it and find a way around it?"

"I'll try, Admiral. Working on it now."

Jeannie sat back with a wolfish grin on her face. "I've got you now, you slippery garogs. I've got you now."

"You seem pretty confident the boy can crack it, Jeannie," chuckled her grandfather.

"Doesn't matter, he's already got the key. If he can crack it, excellent, but if he can't we can still use that odd reading to locate the general area, then we have them. We'll smoke them out."

"Smoke them out?"

"Yes, Grandfather, we start dropping bombs in likely places until they show themselves."

"You'd just bomb them from space?"

"Yes. I won't send what few fighters we have into mountainous terrain against unknown numbers of enemies who know the lay of the land. I'll rattle their cage until they show themselves then offer them the chance to surrender."

"All right, let's say that works and they surrender, then what?"

"Then we force them to reveal themselves to the Duraden for what they are, not gods, but parasites. Once the Duraden see them for what they are, they will no longer fear them. The gods will be forced to trade for food, share knowledge and tech in exchange for meat and grain."

"Do you think they'll agree to trade, or will they try to conquer the Duraden?"

"Good point, Grandfather. I guess we'll have to completely disarm them, find their hidden caches of weapons, etc., and destroy them."

"Will that be enough, do you think, Jeannie?"

"It'll have to be, for the alternative is to annihilate them, and I don't want to do that."

"How did we get to this point, anyway?" asked the president of the Passengers Association. "Yes, the Duraden tried to kill you, but failed miserably and are no real threat to us, are they?"

"It's not that I consider the Duraden a threat, Miriam," replied Jeannie. "It was the threat the gods used against the Duraden if they failed. They threatened to release a deadly toxin to destroy them. They have large canisters of the toxin in place on all four planets. We found and destroyed two of them, but who knows how many exist."

"I see your point, Admiral Sorenson, and I applaud your decision. You're right; we can't just raid an inhabited planet then abandon its people to their fate if we can help them."

Just then, Jeannie noticed Morthel gazing at her info pad. "Morthel?"

"It's Brodie, Admiral. He's cracked it and is sending the new sensor settings to Retriever's sensor station. Shall we go back down for another look?"

"Catch a rest, Captain Morthel. First thing tomorrow we'll resume the hunt."

Cornering the Rat

Next morning, Morthel arrived at EX2 to find Brodie showing Ravel how to work the sensors. "You two are here early."

"Good morning, Captain Morthel," smiled Ravel. "Yes, we've been here a while. My friend wanted to double check his figures and to make sure I knew how the machine works."

"Oh, what's up, Brodie?"

"Captain, no matter how this all plays out, Ravel and his people must learn to use and repair some basic tech. If they don't, they'll be easy prey to the so-called gods."

"Brodie, I have to agree with you there. Carry on with what you were doing."

Once the rest of the crew arrived, EX2 launched and returned to the planet, bringing the newly adjusted sensors online. They arrived at Brodie's coordinates and began the search again, Retriever flying nearby with EX4 and F1 on the wings. "Gotcha!" exclaimed Brodie.

"On forward screen."

"Aye, Captain."

The screen came to life showing a series of broad tunnels connecting several large caverns. There were hundreds of life signs and plenty of weapons. "They're powering weapons."

"Shields. Brodie, send those coordinates to F1 and ..." A weapon fired and EX2 was sent spinning out of control. Two more weapons fired, but the fleet was evading and nothing more was hit.

"F1 to EX2, do you hear me?"

"A moment, Admiral. Three, get us on the ground."

"Working," replied SUVI 3 from the pilot's seat as she fought the spinning ship into submission. She managed to get it under control, avoid crashing into a mountain side, and set down on the valley floor. "Ship has landed, Captain," she sighed as she leaned back and rubbed the tension out of her neck.

"Well done, Three. EX2 to Admiral Sorenson."

"Morthel, report."

"We got hit with something, but SUVI 3 got us down intact. Brodie and Three are checking for damage now. We've got a few bumps and bruises, but everybody appears to be in one piece. I'm just happy we left the baby on Reacher today."

"So am I, Morthel. We've got you on sensors now and ... they've fired the weapons again. You see to your ship; I'll deal with this."

"Understood. EX2 out. Okay, Tommy, talk to me."

"You were right, Captain, a few bumps and bruises and a big mess to clean up. We got off lucky."

"Indeed we did. Love those new shields." Morthel stepped outside to see Thirteen, Connie, Dour, and Alec standing guard, ever watchful. Ravel was with Three and Brodie.

"What's the good word, Chief Engineer?"

"We got lucky, Captain. The shields held for the most part. That was a particle beam of some sort and it managed to knock out our stabilizers, our sensor array, and navigation. We've got navigation and sensors back up; the stabilizers will be repaired in about an hour."

"Will you be all right out here in the open that long?"

"I won't like it," replied Brodie, "but I'll manage."

"Good to know. Work fast, I want to get out of here as soon as we can."

While Brodie and SUVI 3 worked feverishly on the repairs, Retriever, EX4, and F1 went on the attack. They made pass after pass while concentrating their attacks heavily at the sources of weapons fire. The enemy guns fell silent long before the repairs to EX2 were completed. The captain was just about to ask for a report when her comm pinged. "Morthel."

"Sessas. You need rescue?"

"We're good, Sessas. We should be up and running in about a half hour."

"No time, Morthel. Assholes incoming. Maybe we come help anyway."

"All assistance greatly appreciated, Captain Sessas. Morthel out. Thirteen, Sessas says we've got incoming."

"I see them, Captain. Dammit, I don't like them having the high ground."

"Nor do I, return to the ship. All personnel back inside the ship."

"Captain, I haven't finished the repairs to the stabilizers."

"There's no time, Brodie, we've got enemies inbound. Three, see if you can get us onto that ridge."

"Captain, without the stabilizers ..."

"I know, Three, it'll be a challenge. Can you do it?"

"I guess we'll find out soon enough. Everybody strap in, this will be a wild ride."

Wild ride was an understatement. The ship lurched and bucked, but the lightning fast reflexes of their SUVI pilot managed it by firing the maneuvering thrusters in mini bursts. "Sorenson to EX2."

"Morthel here," she groaned.

"Morthel, what are you doing? What's the plan?"

"We're denying the enemy the high ground, testing Three's reflexes, and trying to keep my last meal inside my stomach."

Jeannie's chuckle could be heard in her reply. "How's that working for you?"

"Two out of three is acceptable," came the groaned response as F1 landed beside the now steady EX2.

Brodie, Ravel, and Three were already back at the stabilizer repairs when Jeannie and her crew of SUVI spilled out of F1. "Thirteen?"

"Here, Five," came the call from the edge of the bluff. "There they are; looks like about fifty of them, heavily armed."

"A large pack of garogs," she mused.

"How do you want to do this, Five?"

"Let's try reasoning with them; I'd rather not have to kill them if we can avoid it."

"And if they prove as unreasonable as a garog?"

"Then we do it the hard way. Wish me luck."

As Jeannie rose to her feet to expose herself to the oncoming enemy, the heavily armed SUVI spread out and took cover. She spread her arms wide to show she held no weapon, then called out, the small instrument on her uniform enhancing her voice and translating her words.

"Stop where you are. Send one person ahead to negotiate with me. I will advance alone to meet them." A hail of weapon's fire was the only answer. She leaped aside and took cover.

"Friendly bunch of buggers aren't they," chuckled SUVI 9.

"Aren't they just," sighed Jeannie. "All right, the hard way it is. Let them keep coming until they reach that open area right below, then open fire. We'll hold the high ground as long as we can, then close with them if they reach us. Try to keep one or two alive for me to talk to."

"Understood," came a series of replies.

Jeannie just sighed and shook her head as she watched the enemy march out into the open and advance toward the high ledge where the two small ships rested. Her education in battle tactics of the Earalith, coupled with the memories of her Viking ancestor told her this was foolish.

When the advancing soldiers were well out in the open, she gave the signal. Half the enemy numbers were cut down on the first salvo. They tried to return fire or to find cover, but to no avail. Within moments there were barely a dozen left, cowering behind a few protruding rocks. The SUVI weapons fell silent.

"Throw out your weapons and surrender; you will not be harmed," shouted Jeannie.

"You abominations will all be destroyed," was the answer, followed by weapons fire.

"Common sense doesn't appear to be a strong trait of these people, Five," grinned Thirteen. "So, we sneak up on them?"

"Looks like. Nine, lay down some cover fire to keep them entertained, the rest of us will go down for a closer look." SUVI 9 nodded and swept his pulse rifle to the ready position, popping a fresh energy cell into place. He nodded again then opened fire, sweeping the area below where the enemy lay in hiding. The SUVI split up and leaped down the hill.

A few of the enemy below saw them coming and tried to flee. Those creatures were moving far too fast to target with a weapon. It did them no good at all, they were caught and herded back where the remainder of their troops were now lying dead or captured.

"Clear, Nine. Come down and bring some restraints."

"Acknowledged."

"What are you?" came the fear-filled question from one prisoner.

"We are SUVI," replied Jeannie. "What are you?"

"We are the gods."

"You're not gods. What is your species called?"

"We are Paraka," sighed the prisoner.

"Tell me of the weapon that damaged one of our ships. Those weapons have fallen silent, why?"

"They will no longer function; they have been exhausted or destroyed."

"Will more armed men be sent out to attack us?"

"No. The One is aware we have failed, as did the Duraden. He will order the great doors sealed, keep the people safe inside until you go away."

"That's not going to happen. Sorenson to Orca." She got no response. "Orca, this is Admiral Sorenson, please respond." Again no response. "Morthel, are you aboard EX2?"

"Here, Admiral."

"See if you can raise the Orca for me."

"Aye, Admiral." Jeannie waited impatiently until Morthel got back to her. "Admiral, no response from Orca. Vice-Admiral Drake is aboard the Reacher. She says to keep the small ships on the ground until further notice."

"What the hell?? Patch me through to Reacher." A moment later EX2 connected her to Reacher.

"Reacher here, Vice-Admiral Drake speaking."

"Mandy, it's Jeannie. What the hell is going on up there?"

"We've got ships incoming, Orca and Kreenon have gone dark on my orders. You stay on mission, I've got this. Keep the small fighter ships out of sight just in case."

"Mandy ..."

"No, Jeannie, I've got this. Trust me now. Reacher out."

The Gods Approach

Amanda was on the bridge of the Reacher with Captain Moore when the message came in. "Probie to Reacher." That got her attention. The AI probe had been out at the edge of the system, scanning for incoming ships.

"Vice-Admiral Drake here, Probie. What have you got?"

"Five ships incoming, Vice-Admiral Drake. All are armed, but their sensors are weaker. They will not be able to detect a cloaked ship. All ships are of a single design and flying slowly."

"Are you sure they're coming here?"

"Probie is certain. The planets sent out distress signals when we first defeated the robots. Now ships of a similar design approach."

"Well done, Probie. Return to Reacher. Rhonda, get any small ships not with Jeannie back inside. Comms, get me the Orca."

"Reacher calling Orca."

"Orca here, Sheila Singh commanding."

"Sheila, it's Amanda. We've got five incoming, not friendlies. I need you back here on Reacher's port side. Sheila, full shields and go dark, no comms or other communication. I don't want them to know you're here."

"Understood. Going dark." Even as she spoke, the Orca seemed to vanish as she went to full shields. She was back beside the Reacher within moments.

"Comms, get me the Kreenon."

"Aye, Vice-Admiral. Reacher calling the Kreenon, please respond."

"Kreenon here, Ka'Ron commanding."

"Ka'Ron, it's Amanda. We've got incoming. Get your Maccay back and go to full shields. Stay on Reacher's starboard and go silent."

"Understood, Vice-Admiral." The Kreenon turned to face outward and vanished as they went to full shields.

"All right, Rhonda, let's go out to meet our guests."

"Aye, Vice-Admiral. Anita, face the visitors and ahead one quarter light speed."

"One quarter light speed, aye."

"I'm just hoping they can't revive those damned robots."

"Yeah, that would suck," agreed Amanda. "Vice-Admiral Drake to engineering."

"Moira here, Amanda. What's up?"

"We've got incoming ships, unfriendly. You said you can broadcast commands to those robots."

"Aye, we can, but they're without power."

"Understood, but I'd like to have something ready in case our visitors manage to revive them."

"How much time do I have?"

"Two hours tops."

"Dammit. All right, I'll bring something to the bridge. You can broadcast it through comms."

"Broadcasting it is an excellent plan, but Orca is going to be in the best position to use it. As soon as it's ready, get it to Captain Singh. I'll let her know to listen for your alert, you'll have to be fast, she's only going to have time to flicker her communication array on and back off, you'll have to hit that window."

Amanda sighed and stepped back as Rhonda took over the bridge. "Gunner, arm the main cannon. Secondary gunners to your stations, arm all weapons. Main cannon, target that lead ship."

"Weapons armed and target acquired, Captain."

"Excellent, maintain status."

"Aye, Captain."

"And now we wait," sighed Amanda. "Orca, Kreenon, acquire and maintain position 100 meters off Reacher's bow. If they're unreasonable they'll come at us, you can take them from the flanks." There was no response, just a grin and a nod from the Earalith man at the sensors. He had caught the slight flickers as both ships moved ahead of Reacher.

Two hours later they were closing swiftly with the oncoming ships. Amanda stepped forward again. "Comms, ship-to-ship."

"Ship-to-ship, aye. Channel is open."

"Attention approaching ships, this is the Reacher, flagship of the Wandering Fleet. Please respond." She got no answer. Moira appeared on the bridge and passed her a comm patch which she passed on to Rhonda. "Comms, are they receiving me?"

"I believe they are, Vice Admiral."

"All right let me try again. Approaching ships, this is Vice-Admiral Drake aboard the Reacher, please respond." Again, no answer. "Are we within weapons range yet?"

"For the main cannon, yes, but not for the smaller arms," replied Rhonda. "I'm not sure about the Kreenon, but the Orca could reach them from here."

"Okay. Comms, open ship-to-ship again."

"Channel is open, Vice-Admiral."

"Attention approaching ships; cut your engines and slow your speed. Failure to comply will bring consequences. You have ten seconds."

This time she got an answer. "In ten seconds, you'll all be dead."

"They're powering weapons."

"Captain Moore."

"Fire main cannon," barked Rhonda.

The lead ship seemed to implode, as the front was suddenly thrust out through the stern, then it exploded. "Target destroyed, Vice-Admiral."

"Excellent. Comms, open channel."

"Channel is open."

"Attention approaching ships; cut your speed and power down your weapons."

The answer was swift and angry. "You fool. You've used your only weapon. We have four ships to your one. Surrender and prepare to be boarded. Attack speed."

"Shields!"

"Shields at full, Captain."

"Dammit," snarled Amanda. "Orca, Kreenon, attack! Reacher, back off, stay out of weapons range unless we have no other option."

To the horror of the oncoming ships, devastating weapons fire came from nowhere. These people obviously had cloaked ships; that much became apparent when the one ship they could detect vanished from their sensors.

The enemy ships began to return fire, but without any clear target, they sprayed missiles and laser fire at random. Enough missiles hit the Orca's shields to give then a hint and they concentrated their attack on that spot. It did them no good at all, the big ship was far more maneuverable and suffered no damage, although she inflicted a great deal as did the Kreenon.

Suddenly the escape pods of one ship flashed out into space to be picked up by another. Not all managed to reach it.

Another ship released a number of robotic fighters, but Sheila broadcast the kill codes developed by Moira to shut them off. It worked and the robots hung useless in space. Orca and Kreenon focused their fire on a single ship, and it exploded, then a second ship exploded, and then a third, until only a single ship was left.

The sudden squawk of the comms brought an end to the battle. "Stop, stop, we surrender, we surrender."

"Cease fire!"

At that command, the rain of hellfire stopped, and the wounded ship hung in space at an awkward angle. The one ship reappeared in space as the voice returned to them. "Power down your weapons, now."

"They're powering down, Vice-Admiral."

"Thank you, sensors. Comms, ship-to-ship."

"Ship-to-ship, aye. Channel is open, Vice-Admiral."

"Enemy ship, power down your engines and assemble your personnel in an open area. All personnel to be unarmed. Do you understand?"

"We understand."

"They're powering down the engines, Vice-Admiral."

"All right. Rhonda, have Security ready to receive guests. I want them all transported over and locked in the brig."

"I doubt our brig will hold a full ship's crew, but we'll try," said Rhonda, as she nodded to Jake.

"I'll let Kar know what's coming," he chuckled. "Hal's missing all the fun. Captain, perhaps the Orca could accommodate any overflow we might have for the brig."

"We're being hailed, Vice-Admiral."

"Put them through."

"This is the crew of the Dorgod. All are assembled as required. We are ready to die."

"Good for you, but it won't happen today. You'll be transported to our ships and held prisoner until the Admiral decides what to do with you. Everyone stand still."

It took nearly a half hour to get them all, and in the end thirty of them were sent to the Orca. "We've got them all, Vice-Admiral."

"Thank you, Captain Moore. As soon as the cannon is ready, blast that damned ship to oblivion. I'll inform the fleet we're returning to our original position as soon as that's done."

"Aye, Vice-Admiral. Gunner."

"Target destroyed, Captain."

"Thank you, Gunner, stand down weapon."

"Weapon at rest, Captain."

"We're ready, Vice-Admiral."

"Well done. Comms, ship-to-ship."

"Channel is open, Vice-Admiral."

"Orca, Kreenon, well done. Return to your original position."

"Acknowledged," came both replies.

"Rhonda, send Probie back out to keep watch for any more guests, then return to original position. Once we're under way, I'm ready for a tea and cake break."

"Agreed," chuckled Rhonda. "I'd suggest something stronger, but we're both still on duty."

Amanda smiled and nodded at that. She reached for her comm unit. "Amanda Drake to Miriam Holbrooke."

The president of the Passenger's Association was quick to respond. "Miriam here, Amanda. Dare I ask what's going on?"

"Meet me at Simple Pleasures in ten minutes and I'll fill you in."

"I'll be there. Miriam out."

"Ready, Rhonda?"

"I'm ready. Anita, the bridge is yours."

Laying Siege

While Amanda took command of the fleet and dealt with the incoming ships, Jeannie led her ground forces as they closed in on the enemy stronghold. It was locked down even as she'd been told. The heavy steel blast doors were impervious to any of the weapons she had available, she'd need the Orca to cut them open.

"They've gone to ground all right," mused Thirteen.

"Yes, and there's not a damned thing we can do until the ships get back."

"You seem unhappy, do you not believe the Vice-Admiral knows what she's doing?"

Jeannie sighed and sank to a cross-legged position on the ground, staring at the huge metal barrier between her and her prey. Thirteen sat beside her. "Oh, she knows what she's doing, Thirteen."

"Worried about her? Protective instincts driving you crazy?"

Jeannie chuckled at that. "Yes to both. I confess I tend to be a bit of a mother hen."

"Five, you're the herd leader; I'd be concerned if you weren't concerned. EX2 was in trouble, and you were right there to face the predators. The skies were clear when we launched this morning; otherwise, I'm sure you'd have kept the fleet together.

"Five, I served the Vice-Admiral when she captained the Explorer and again on EX2. The woman is smart, and cool under fire, yet takes no chances unnecessarily. If she says she's got it then she truly believes she has it under control."

"I'm not doubting that, Thirteen, it's just that I know what she's doing."

"Oh?"

"We couldn't raise the Orca, and I'll bet we'd have had no luck if we'd tried the Kreenon either. Mandy's setting the Reacher out as bait with the two warships, fully shielded, flying on her flank. She'll try to talk sense to the visitors, but if it doesn't work Sheila and Ka'Ron will cut them to ribbons."

"And that's bad because?"

"It's not bad, old friend, it's exactly what I'd have done."

"But?"

"But it should be me."

"Let me guess, you'd have cloaked the Reacher then led the Orca and Kreenon out in F1, right?"

"Absolutely right. I'd have protected the home ship, not risk it in battle."

"Spoken like a true SUVI," chuckled Thirteen. "However, the Vice-Admiral isn't SUVI, she's human, and they're a fierce lot when you provoke them. I'll bet F1 has fully trained her in Earalithian battle tactics."

"He has, and you're right, she can be fierce when provoked. Do me a favor?"

"Just give me a minute." He closed his eyes and drew in a deep breath. A few moments later he opened his eyes again, they were glowing amber. "You'll hear from her soon. The Vice-Admiral was successful, and the Reacher will be back in position before nightfall."

Jeannie sighed and relaxed her shoulders. "Good to know. We'll wait until the big ships return before we smoke these buggers out. Let's get back to our ships. We'll go into orbit and await the return of the warships."

They returned to EX2 and F1 to find Retriever and EX4 there as well. "Captain Morthel, your ship's status?"

"All repairs complete, Admiral. EX2 ready for duty."

"Excellent. People, we can do no more here at the moment. For now, we'll go back to orbit and keep a watchful eye on the prey. Once the Reacher has returned, we'll go home for a rest then come back with a new plan. Back to your ships."

The small ships returned to space to await the arrival of Reacher and company. Aboard EX2, Brodie felt eyes on him and turned to see Thirteen grinning. "What?"

"I'm damn proud of you, Brodie."

"Oh? Why?"

"Why? We were outside for hours, and you were out there working on the repairs the whole time. Even when the ship was up on that ridge, you stayed with it. I even saw you look up from time to time, gazing out over the long sight lines. That took courage and strength."

"It's all Ravel's fault; he made me do it."

Thirteen chuckled at that. "The support of a friend always helps, but in the end, it was you who did the deed. How did it feel when you looked out over those mountains?"

"I nearly crapped myself. It turned my guts to jelly, I nearly lost my stomach contents, and then I started to black out. I brought my eyes back to the side of the ship until I settled down then tried again. It was still scary as hell, but a bit easier the second time."

"Like Thirteen said, Brodie, we're all extremely proud of you," agreed Morthel. "That took courage and more."

Brodie blushed and looked away shyly. Ravel grinned and lightly gripped his shoulder. "Yes indeed, my friend here is tougher than he looks." This did nothing to relieve Brodie's embarrassment.

* * * * *

Reacher returned and the small ships swept inside. The crews dispersed to the mess for a meal and to their quarters for a rest. Amanda flew into Jeannie's arms, but slowly released her and stepped back. "Jeannie, what's wrong?"

"Nothing at all, sweet Mandy, I'm just tired."

"Bullshit, Jeannie Sorenson. Think about who you're talking to; I can read you like an open book. Let's not do this with an audience; your office or our quarters?"

"Mandy ..."

Amanda sighed and allowed her shoulders to relax. "All right, quarters then. Come on." She took Jeannie by the hand and led her away to their quarters.

"That didn't look good," mused SUVI 20, as they watched them walk away.

"Domestic dispute," said Sessas. "Two ways to do same thing, SUVI way, human way. Amanda fix, all good. You go home, snuggle Jake, say love from Sessas."

"You're right as usual, sister Sessas. See you tomorrow."

* * * * *

Jeannie followed Amanda into their quarters and stopped just inside the door. "Mandy ..."

Amanda turned with fire in her eyes. "Go ahead, say it."

"Mandy, please don't be so upset. I'm not angry."

"Just disappointed in me?"

"Disappointed that you'd risk the Reacher and everyone on board unnecessarily. I don't understand why, and I don't understand why you're so upset."

Amanda slowly let her shoulders relax and the fire left her eyes. "I'm upset that when I hugged you, you were stiff, cold, and obviously disapproving. It hurt, Jeannie, more than you know. It told me you were angry with me, that you disapproved of the way I've handled things.

"It hurt that you didn't even seem pleased or relieved that I was still alive, that I'd succeeded, led the fleet against superior numbers and defeated them with no casualties or damage. You didn't even ask me what happened, or what I had done or why. You judged me and my actions without giving me a hearing."

The eyes of the SUVI warrior had gone a deep amber, but she forced her defensiveness back. She sighed deeply as her eyes returned to green. "You're entirely right about that, Mandy, all of it, and I'm sorry for it. I am." Suvi-Jean sighed deeply and looked into her lover's eyes. "Please give me a chance to suck up and make it right."

In spite of herself, Amanda started to grin. She could never stay angry at Jeannie, nor did she want to. "How about I give you a full report instead? Come, sit with me in the cuddling chair and I'll tell all."

Jeannie relaxed into the oversized chair and Amanda sat on the arm and pulled her close. "You had just seen the ground troops going after Morthel and you went to her defense. The other ships were busy trying to knock out the enemy weapons.

"That's when Probie came back to report five ships incoming from the direction the ground enemy had signaled for help. I suspected that's who it was. Probie had scanned them and found they were the same technology as the robots and with similar weapons.

"I called the two warships, told them to fly Reacher's wings and go dark, then went out to meet our guests."

"But the Reacher ..."

"Hush, I'm getting there. Earalith battle tactics, remember? The Reacher has our most powerful weapon with the longest reach. She's also our biggest ship. I hoped her sheer size might deter the enemy, but it didn't.

"I tried to negotiate with them, but all I got was, 'You're all going to die, you're an abomination, we will destroy you all.' That sort of thing. When I realized it was no use, I commanded the Reacher to take out the lead ship, hoping that would shake their resolve. It didn't.

"Again they said 'we're going to kill you all'; I ordered the Reacher to drop back and the Orca and Kreenon to attack. At no point did the Reacher ever get within range of their weapons. As she backed off, Rhonda went to full shields, and we disappeared from their sensors. The Orca and Kreenon destroyed three of the remaining ships and the last one surrendered.

"We transported the survivors to our brig and Orca's, destroyed that last ship, and then returned to you."

Jeannie snuggled deeper into Amanda's embrace. "You did right, Mandy, all of it. Now tell me what you're not telling me. Why didn't you call for me, you had time?"

"Because I know you, Suvi-jean. You'd have ordered the Reacher to stay behind and led off with F1, trying to protect the Reacher and her people. You'd have been well inside the range of their weapons before you could deal with them. You'd be out there under fire without your biggest weapon. I wasn't about to let you risk yourself unnecessarily, besides you had your hands full planet-side.

"Now, you tell me what you're not telling me. Your mood was too cold when you arrived, I knew it was more than me that had rubbed your fur the wrong way."

"It's those people, Mandy, the self-proclaimed gods. They're so damned unreasonably stupid. Even when it is painfully obvious they're out matched, they just keep repeating the dogma and marching forward. We killed dozens of them and there was no need for it. Now those who remain are hiding behind heavy blast doors and we need the Orca's forward laser weapon to cut through it."

"We could leave them in there, bottle them up inside."

"We could, but they'd starve to death eventually."

"There's more, tell me all of it."

"I don't understand them, Mandy. I don't understand what happened here in the past, and I don't understand why they refuse to adapt or compromise. In the face of certain defeat, wouldn't you surrender to keep as many of your people alive as possible?"

"I would, and so would you, but apparently not these people, and that's driving you crazy, isn't it? You're a natural survivor, and this blatant disregard for basic survival makes no sense to you at all."

"Yeah, that's about the size of it, all right. What should we do now, do you think?"

"Beats me. Question some of the prisoners maybe, see if we can talk sense to any of them."

Jeannie sighed and rose to her feet. "That's as good a plan as any, let's go."

"The only place you're going is to the mess for a meal, then back here for a rest. Nothing else is likely to happen before tomorrow."

"All right, Mandy, I bow to your better judgment."

Amanda took her arm and led her toward the mess hall. "I was right about the battle tactics you'd have used, wasn't I?"

"Yes, you were."

"And you'd have left me on Reacher to protect me, wouldn't you?"

"Yes. I can't help it, Mandy, I'm quite protective of you."

"I know, so why does it piss you off so bad when I protect you?"

"Because I'm the big scary SUVI who's supposed to protect everybody."

"And nobody's allowed to protect you?"

"Nobody ever has ... until now."

"Yeah? So, how does it feel?"

"It's nice, kind of sweet, but Mandy ..."

"I know, honey, not if it risks the rest of the people."

"But you will do it again ..."

"Of course I will, you know that."

"I know, Mandy. You've always protected me, even from myself. I love you for that."

"Then my world is perfect."

Interview with an Enemy

The next morning the captains and passenger reps met in the briefing room of the Reacher. "Everybody's here, Admiral."

"Thank you, Vice-Admiral. Report."

"All was quiet yesterday aboard the Reacher. Our non-combat ships were aboard while you led the fighter ships against the enemy. Things were busy on the planet when Probie reported five ships incoming. Since you were leading our forces on the planet, I took the fleet and engaged the incoming enemy ships.

"I tried to reason with them, but to no avail, so we engaged. Result, no damage to the fleet, all five enemy ships destroyed, and a number of enemy taken prisoner. Several of those are here aboard the Reacher and still more on the Orca.

"Thank you, Vice-Admiral. Rhonda, report."

Captain Moore chuckled at that. "Aye, Admiral. Reacher led the fleet to meet the oncoming ships. Our shields were down to keep us visible while Orca and Kreenon were fully cloaked. We remained well out of the enemy weapons' range while the Vice-Admiral tried to reason with them.

"When it became clear there was no other option except battle, the Vice-Admiral ordered the main cannon fired, then the Reacher went to full shields and withdrew while the Orca and Kreenon engaged and defeated the enemy."

"Your assessment, Captain Moore?"

"I greatly admire the Vice-Admiral's patience, Admiral, for she gave them more chances than I would have, and yet, she kept the Reacher, and her inhabitants well back out of the fight. As in the battle with the Wrax, the main cannon was used to weaken the enemy, then the fighting ships took over.

"Any time you're busy elsewhere, I'm more than happy to have the Vice-Admiral in command of the fleet."

"Sheila?"

"I agree fully with Rhonda. The Vice-Admiral is an able leader, cool headed and decisive under fire."

"Ka'Ron?"

"I agree as well."

"As do I," grinned Jeannie, as she stopped pacing and settled into her chair. "Well, Mandy, you've had your trial by fire, now give us your assessment. If you could go back and do it again, what, if anything, would you do differently?"

"Nothing, Admiral. I led the fleet out to meet them and to represent our combined species if they would consider discussion or negotiation, but they refused. When it was clear they wouldn't, I ordered the attack and stepped away to let the captains deal with it."

"You didn't direct the battle?"

"What was needed was quite clear, and for me to interfere with the captains at that point would be less than helpful. They knew what to do and did it efficiently, making my job easy."

"You wouldn't keep trying to get through to them?"

"No, Admiral. SUVI 20's encounter with a single-minded fool, and the required solution was my guide."

"When the leader wouldn't listen to reason you hit him with a hammer?"

"Exactly."

There were chuckles all around and Twenty shook a finger at Amanda. Jeannie smiled as she agreed. "Yes, that encounter is an excellent guide to follow under those circumstances.

"Now we move to the next step. We have those people, called the Paraka, on the ground bottled up in their caverns, they're fine for now. We also have a number of Paraka prisoners that Amanda gathered up. I want to talk to a few of them, see if I can learn anything useful."

"Admiral, may I ask what is your long-term goal here?" said Miriam Holbrooke, the passenger representative.

"Miriam our goal here is to disarm these Paraka so they can no longer harm the Duraden. The Duraden befriended us; the Paraka ordered our deaths and insisted on that objective. Before we leave this system, I want to be sure the two peoples are able to function on equal terms.

"Also, I confess I'm deeply curious to understand how this came to be as it is. Obviously the Duraden were, at one time, an advanced people, having populated four planets in this system. Somehow, they encountered the Paraka, and war erupted between them.

"At this point, I assume it was the Paraka who found this system and conquered it, but the lore speakers of the Duraden tell of a time when the Duraden welcomed the visitors and offered to share great knowledge with them."

"And you're consumed with curiosity as to what actually happened, right?" chuckled her grandfather.

"In a word, yes," admitted Jeannie. "That, and I want to make sure it doesn't happen again as soon as we leave. However, I'd like your input, all of you."

"We should stay, finish job," said Captain Sessas.

"What she said," agreed SUVI 20.

One by one the other captains joined in. It was clear they were as curious as she was.

"Miriam?"

"I'm with you on this one, Admiral. It's quite a puzzle and perhaps the folks in the brig can supply a few answers."

"So, we all agree to stay and finish this. All right then, Rhonda, have somebody see if they can find a leader or officer of the Paraka relaxing in your brig."

Captain Moore pointed at Hal White who reached for his comm. "Hal to Kar."

"Kar here, Commander."

"Kar, see if you can find an officer or leader among our guests in the brig then haul his sorry butt to the briefing room."

"On it, Commander."

It wasn't a long wait. Sub-Commander Karissa Glenn soon arrived with a uniformed Paraka in tow, two security guards flanking him. They marched him in front of Suvi-jean. "This one claims to have been the captain of the last ship, Admiral."

"Thank you, Sub-Commander. All right, you, what is your name?"

The only answer she got was a sneer. The creature turned to Captain Baris. "Is there no true man among you? I will not stoop to treating with a female."

The expected explosion did not come. The admiral's eyes flashed amber, then slowly returned to green as a smile teased at her lips. She took a step back and spoke. "All yours, Hal."

Hal nodded and approached the green-skinned creature. Tilting his head slightly to the side, he inspected what stood before him. The Paraka was about even with his height, green-skinned with small scales covering all exposed skin. The eyes were almost black and well hooded with a thick eyebrow ridge, the nose flat and broad, and the skull hairless. Each arm held a six fingered hand with an opposable thumb, all fully scaled.

"Well, slave of the females, speak."

The creature didn't see the blow coming, it was so swiftly delivered. He fell to the floor, gasping for air. Hal grabbed it by the loose skin at its neck and jerked it back to its feet. "Did I ask you to speak, specimen? No? Then you will remain silent.

"I'm not sure this slug will have any useful knowledge, Admiral. We should send it to the dissection chamber, perhaps it might be edible."

Jeannie grinned and nodded to her grandfather who winked at her. "You could be right, Commander White, but give it a try anyway, then we'll decide what to do with it."

"Aye, Captain Baris, as you command." Hal turned back to the creature, a hard look in his eye. It took an involuntary step back away from him, but the security guard was there to push him back to the waiting Hal. Hal sighed deeply, as though about to attempt an unpleasant task. "You commanded one of the ships who came to defeat us, yes?"

"Yes," came the shaky reply. The arrogance had left the creature.

"How many ships were there? How many ships do your people have? How many will they send here?"

"There are thousands, all will respond to our distress signals."

Hal chuckled at that. "They'll all face the same fate, you know. Did you see how many ships you faced?"

"No. At first there was only one, but it vanished, and we were destroyed by unseen forces."

"And so you have faced a small portion of our fleet. Now stop lying and tell me the truth, how many more ships do your people have to send against us?"

The creature began to tremble slightly and deflate, all bravado gone. "None. All ships were sent to protect the outposts. The demons must be contained at all cost."

"Why?"

"The One has declared it. It has always been this way since the demon worlds were discovered by the glorious ancestors. The One declared them too evil to be allowed to exist. Our people tried to eradicate them, but some managed to survive. The ancestors confined them, preventing them from escaping and preventing any other from helping them."

"What is the One?"

The creature looked utterly perplexed. "The One is the One. The one who rules all, commands all, knows all, creates all, is all that is."

Hal sighed. "So, the One is your god. How do you know what his commands truly are? How does the One communicate with you?"

"Through our commanders, of course."

"Zealots," muttered Hal, as he began to pace before the prisoner. "All right, we'll let that be as it is for now. You say there are no more ships like the one you commanded."

"Yes. They were the last and the means to make more has been lost."

"Explain."

"Long ago, during the war with the demons, the world was great, and mighty things were wrought. The One arose to ultimate command and sent the people against the demons, to utterly destroy them. Our priest could tell you more of this."

"Your priest? It survived and is here?"

"No, the voice of the One was not brought to this ship with the rest."

"Then he's got to be on the Orca," said Jeannie, pointing a finger at Sheila. A few moments later Sheila grinned and let her hand drop away from her comm. "Ellen's bringing him over now, Admiral."

"Excellent." Even as she spoke there was a tap on the door. "Enter."

Ellen Brady, chief of security on the Orca, ushered a rather disheveled Paraka into the room. "Here he is, Admiral."

"He looks a little unhappy, Ellen. Did you have trouble convincing him to join us?"

"When I found him, the lot of them were on their knees praying to him. He was unhappy to be interrupted, especially by a woman. He ordered them to attack me. Nineteen and the lads had to restore order. End result, here's your guy."

"Well done, Ellen," chuckled Jeannie. "Hal, please continue to gather information from these people."

Hal nodded then approached the priest. He gazed at the arrogant creature who glared back. "Tell me of the One."

The priest gazed at him for a moment then started to speak. "The One is the true provider, all blessings flow from ..."

"Not that rhetoric nonsense, save that for the fools who'll actually believe it. Tell me of the One, who was he? What was he? When did he exist?"

"He exists everywhere ..."

He got no further as Hal's hand on his throat choked off the speech. "I told you, not that doctrine, not that crap. Tell me who he was, what he was, how he came to be a god." He thrust the creature away, but Ellen shoved him back.

Terrified, the creature looked to his captain, but the man would not meet his eyes. "Tell him what he wants to know, or you'll get us all killed." The priest swallowed hard and began.

"Long, long ago our people were many, but fractured, we had no purpose except to destroy each other. The One was a great leader of the military, and he conquered all who opposed him. He gave the people direction, and the great ships were built, ten in all, one for each tribe of the Paraka under his rule.

"The ships set out to explore but found nothing useful within the sphere of our world, our sun. In his infinite wisdom the One sent the ships out to explore the stars, and this system was found. The people of this system were many and their worlds were fruitful. The people welcomed the Children of the One and our ancestors believed they could bring them under the guidance of the One, but no.

"The scum of these worlds refused the blessing of the One's guidance, claiming their way was better for all, that instead of all things being given for the glory of the One, that all should be shared equally. Imagine, a slave being given an equal share of food as a captain or a Speaker of the One!

"Word was taken back to the One who ordered them all destroyed, and their worlds quarantined. While the soldiers of the One began the destruction, the guardians were built. It took most of the metal available to our people to create them, but it was done. They were brought here and released to enforce the quarantine.

"A base of observation was established on each of the four worlds and the holy volunteers were sent to release the gas of death upon the demons should any manage to survive. Generations passed and nothing was heard from the volunteers and knowledge of them, and their purpose, was forgotten by all except the priesthood.

"Sadly, all knowledge of building or repairing the great ships was lost as well. The five were housed in a museum, but, for some reason they suddenly awakened. Some of the volunteers had managed to survive and their descendants were calling for aid, the guardians had been defeated. The elite of our military were sent aboard the ships which then launched on their own. None knew how to operate them, but the ships were guided by the power of the One. The rest you know."

Hal White sighed and turned to the Admiral. "Jeannie?"

"Well done, Hal. Well, people, that explains part of our mystery. Morthel, do you still have your Duraden guests on EX2?"

"Actually, Admiral, they're on the Reacher. Since we were going into a possible battle situation, I left them with Dr. Reilly. He seems to have a strong rapport with the lorespeakers. Dour and Ravel did fly with us, but the rest remained here."

"Good thinking, Morthel. Sorenson to the chief of medical research."

"Eamon here, Jeannie. What's up?"

"We've got a brig full of a new species for you to check out, and I need your two lore speaker friends here in the briefing room."

"I'll drop them off on my way to the brig. Eamon out."

"This should prove interesting," mused Jeannie. "I doubt any of the Duraden have ever laid eyes on one of their gods before. Kar, would you take these two characters back to cells please."

"Of course, Admiral. Bring them." The security guards took the two creatures and guided them out the door just as the two lore speakers arrived.

"You wanted to speak with us, great Admiral?"

"Yes, Garanan. You and Ordain have told us of a time long ago when the strangers came from the skies. You spoke of how they were friendly, but then attacked. Have you ever seen one of those people, the ones who call themselves your gods?"

"No, Admiral, we never see them, only hear their voices."

"We captured a number of them, Garanan. Watch now while they speak of that time long ago." At her nod, Amanda hit the button for the playback. A holographic scene appeared over the table, and they watched as Hal interviewed the Paraka. The faces of the two women grew dark as they listened.

Garanan fairly shook with outrage as the interview finished. "Scum? This is why they destroyed our ancestors, because our ways were different? Because we shared the bounty of life with all? That was the dangerous knowledge that a lorespeaker was forbidden to know?"

"Apparently it was," sighed Jeannie. "I suspect there is more to learn here, Garanan. Those two were from the home world of the Paraka, a world that is no longer a threat to you. However, the Paraka on the ground, those who pretend to be your gods, have more to tell. They will have more knowledge of the passing generations that those two did not."

With an effort, Garanan got control of her emotions. "Great Admiral, may I make a request?"

"Of course, my friend. What do you need?"

"Is there a way I can share this with the rest of my people? My own clan will trust my words, but the others may not. If possible, I would also like to confront one of these gods."

"We will give you a copy of that interview to take home with you, you as well, Ordain. Also, once we dig out those false gods, you both will be invited to join us when we interview them. Further, we will help you take your message to the Duraden people of the rest of the lost worlds."

Digging out the Rats

EX2 had been orbiting above the Paraka stronghold all night. As the alarm sounded at the beginning of the day shift, Morthel stepped from her sleeping booth. "Thirteen, anything moving down there?"

"Nothing moving, Captain, at least, nothing we can detect."

"I think I've got it, Captain."

"Brodie?"

"The frequency to penetrate that giant bunker with sensors, Captain. Just a ... there, putting it up on the forward screen."

"All right, what exactly am I looking at, Brodie?"

"The inside of the bunker, Captain. Everything looks gray, that's because of their shielding. The darker spots moving around are life signs. The red are weapons signatures. They're massed to defend the gate; all weapons are in that area."

"F1 has landed, Captain."

"Thank you, Lilly. Shall we go down and inform the admiral of what we've found?" EX2 swept in and landed beside F1, the hatch was opened and Morthel stepped out. Smiling, she led the way. They found Jeannie and her SUVI crew standing at the edge of the ridge gazing down at the huge metal doors. Hal, SUVI 20, and Captain Sessas were there as well. "Good morning, Admiral."

"Good morning, Captain Morthel. Tell me good things."

"Brodie broke the sensor block they have up, Admiral. They've amassed all the weapons and fighters close to the gate for defense, the others are well back in the caverns."

"Good to know."

"The Orca is in position, Admiral," said Hal. "What's the battle plan? Have the Orca shoot open the doors then rush them?"

"I'd rather talk them out. Actually, what I meant is, I want you to talk them out."

"Yeah, they have a real thing about a woman in command, don't they?"

"They have that in common with my own people," sighed Morthel.

"Yeah, well, I don't," chuckled Hal. "Okay, how's this supposed to work?"

"Linsey should be here in a moment with some toys and a few guests."

"Guests?"

"The two you interviewed yesterday and Grandfather."

"Okay, sounds good to me. Here comes Friendship now."

The small scout ship swept in and landed lightly beside EX2. Linsey da Silva and SUVI 18 stepped out followed by Captain Baris of Recovery Two, and the two Paraka under guard. "Good morning, Admiral."

"Linsey, what have you brought us?"

"We've got a loudspeaker system that should penetrate to the enemy, plus I tweaked the translator to accommodate a few more Paraka words and phrases."

"How long have you been at this?"

"Since the first one appeared on the Reacher," grinned Eighteen. "She's been driving Marcus nuts trying to keep her back and out of harm's way in his overcrowded brig."

"Well, with any luck we'll empty out that brig today. All yours, Grandfather, Hal."

"What's the endgame?" asked Captain Baris.

"Kill as few of them as possible," replied Jeannie.

"Understood." He conferred with Hal for a moment then passed the loudspeaker to Hal, who plugged it in to his translator unit.

Hal turned it up to max then spoke. "Attention, all Paraka inside the caverns, attention all Paraka inside the caverns. You are surrounded by experienced warriors with superior weapons. Surrender and no harm will come to you." He gave it a few moments then repeated the message. Still nothing.

"Attention Paraka commanders, I know you're holding out for reinforcements from the home world. That rescue will not come. Yesterday that fleet met our own fleet and was destroyed. There is no help coming for you; you're alone, outnumbered, and out gunned. Surrender now and save your people."

Finally he got an answer. "You lie, demon. You will all be dead before the next sunrise."

"Tell me you didn't release the gas. You have to know by now that it will not harm us."

"It will kill you all."

"Stubborn fool," muttered Hal.

"He's just going on what he's always been taught," said Captain Baris. "He's trying to stall, waiting for the rescue fleet."

"Yeah, that's not going to happen. Jeannie, perhaps our guests should have a word with him." She nodded so he pulled the Paraka captain closer and motioned to the loudspeaker. "Speak to those people, tell them what happened to your fleet."

"People of Morak, hear my words. I am Torada of Parak, one of five captains who left the home world to come to your aid."

"If this is true, why do you stand beside the enemy and not kill them?"

"I stand here because they defeated the guardians, and they defeated the fleet. I and the other few survivors were taken prisoner. We were unable to kill them, and they have refused to kill us. They do not wish to kill you. Open the gates and surrender, none will be harmed if you comply."

"Lies, all lies. I don't know who or what you are, but no Paraka would ever defy the commands of the One. The law of the One clearly states all who come here must die, none may leave alive."

"This is getting us nowhere," sighed Jeannie. "Bloody fools." She reached for her comm. "Sorenson to Captain Singh."

"Here, Admiral."

"Is the Orca in position?"

"We are."

"Open that damned door for me, would you?"

"With pleasure, Admiral. Stand back, this'll get hot."

Jeannie motioned her people back as a thin line of pure hellfire lanced from the Orca to strike the massive gate. In mere moments it began to glow red, then white, then it melted down into a puddle of molten metal. The great gate was down, and the interior of the stronghold exposed.

Jeannie chuckled as a hail of weapons fire came from the interior but hit nothing. The heat from the melting gate had driven them back and all they could do was shoot out through the hole where the gate once stood.

"So what now?" asked Captain Baris. "Do we attack?"

"No, that area needs to cool down for a while before we can get in or they can get out," replied Jeannie. "Morthel, can you reach inside with your transporter now?"

"I'll check," she grinned, reaching for her comm. "Morthel to Lilly."

"Here, Captain."

"Lilly, check your transporter and see if you can grab somebody from inside and drop them beside me for the admiral."

"Working."

A few moments later a Paraka appeared right in front of Jeannie. She grabbed him and tossed him toward Hal who shoved him to SUVI 20 who placed him in restraints. At Jeannie's nod Hal spoke to the terrified man. "The One does not rule here, we do. We do not want to harm you, but your people must surrender. Go back and tell them that."

Hal winked at Morthel, who gave the order. The man in restraints vanished in a flash of light to reappear back inside where he had originally been standing. A few moments later there was a great barrage of weapons fire from inside, but again, no harm was done. The men inside had a limited field of vision and no targets.

"I guess he delivered the message, but they didn't like it, Admiral."

"Apparently not. All right, we up the game. Sorenson to Orca and Reacher. I want as many security people down here as you can spare."

"Acknowledged," came the two replies. A moment later security people began to appear on the ground.

When all had arrived, Jeannie spoke to them. "Listen up. We're going to start transporting as many of the enemy as possible out of there. Your task is to grab them, disarm and restrain them, before they can do any harm.

"Sorenson to all ships, begin transporting the Paraka out of the caverns and drop them beside our security forces.'"

Hal and Ellen Brady swiftly spread out their forces creating an open space between them. As soon as a Paraka appeared he was stunned then put in restraints. It was a scene of pure mayhem as the Paraka began to appear faster than the security forces could deal with. A few got off a shot, one security man was hit, but the armor protected him.

SUVI 19 waded through the dazed Paraka arriving like some sort of machine, ignoring the blows, and shaking off a couple of hits from a weapon. He tossed them toward waiting officers, stripped away weapons, and more.

Finally there were no more combatants arriving, but the elders, females, and young continued to appear. They no longer tried to put them in restraints, just herded them to an open space and told them to wait.

The flow of prisoners slowed to a trickle then stopped. The sun was well on its way to the horizon by this time. Recovery One landed and spilled out two crews. The first began to rig lighting while the second approached the open doorway and began spraying coolant on the still glowing metal. When it had cooled, Olga Volkov approached Jeannie.

"Looks like it's safe to enter now, Admiral. Sensors say the place is empty, but who knows for sure."

"Hmm. Let's find out, shall we? Sessas, send in your strikers. Tell them to destroy any weapons they find, destroy any form of comms and transporters. Leave them with all their life support systems."

"Sessas to ship."

"Billy here, Captain."

"Billee, take strikers, go in, destroy weapons, comms, transporters. Leave life support systems."

"Understood."

"Billee."

"Yes, Captain?"

"Bring out Warhammer, Tentee getting bored."

Jeannie smiled as she heard his laughing reply. "Aye, Captain. Warmaiden to accompany the strike force. Understood."

As the strikers arrived and passed the Warhammer to SUVI 20, Jeannie noticed the pilot of EX4 and the medic from Recovery One in an animated conversation. Both kept glancing her way as they spoke. The next time they glanced up she crooked a finger at them.

"Come on, Ebony, you know I'm right."

"Yes, I agree with you completely, but we'll need the admiral's permission to start, then we need Captain Moore and Merriam Holbrooke on side, then ..." The admiral was signaling them to approach. Ebony took Brie by the arm and led her over to Jeannie.

"All right, you two, what's going on?"

Ebony matched her grin as she replied. "Admiral, Brie here has just pointed out a huge problem for us, and better yet, she's come up with the solution."

"Talk to me, Ensign Elliot."

Blushing, Brie poked Ebony lightly in the ribs then made her pitch to the admiral. "Ma'am, this has been a hugely successful day, but it presents a problem. There are hundreds of prisoners now, many are women and children. They're confused, terrified, cold, and hungry. We'll need to do something for them soon."

Jeannie nodded as she realized the girl was right. She'd been completely focused on capturing these people without annihilating them in the process. "Agreed and thank you for bringing this to my attention. What's your solution?"

"Well, ma'am, the kitchens on the Reacher could easily make food packages, stores could provide blankets, and we could find lots of volunteers among the passengers to help distribute them."

"Indeed they could; I like it. So, Ebony, what's your stake in this?"

Ebony blushed deeply as she saw the admiral's grin. Getting into the game, Brie spoke up. "Oh, we need Ebony to organize it, Admiral. She has plenty of contacts among the passengers and ..."

"Of course, you're right, Brie, is it? Yes, Brie, you'll need Ebony's help. All right, the task is yours. Ebony, you're temporarily assigned to Brie, help her make this happen. Ladies, all fun aside, you're quite right about this and I had overlooked it. I'll let Rhonda know you're coming."

Jeannie turned to Captain Baris. "Grandfather, Brie and Ebony have a special mission of mercy and they'll need a ship with plenty of cargo space."

"Recovery Two has empty holds right now," he smiled. "Let's go, ladies."

Captain Baris led them to his ship which lifted off soon after they arrived. As the ship rose Jeannie was on the comms. "Sorenson to Vice-Admiral Drake."

"Here, Jeannie."

"Mandy, find Rhonda and Mirriam, then meet Recovery Two. Ebony and her friend have a mighty task and will need their help."

"Understood."

While Amanda gathered up the president of the passenger's association and the captain of the Reacher and headed for the launch bay, Brie was laying out her task for Captain Baris and his first officer, Chance Morita.

Captain Baris smiled and nodded as she finished. "She's right, Chance. What do you think?"

"Miriam will find the volunteers all right, the kitchens and stores can handle the supplies, but we'll need to scrounge a few things."

"Oh? Like what?" asked Brie.

"Tables for one thing," he replied. "You'll also need waste collection receptacles and a few more odd bits."

"Oh. I hadn't thought of any of that."

Chance Morita grinned as he winked at her and turned to the captain. "What do you think, Sir, shall we take care of that for her?"

"Absolutely," smiled the captain. "Leave that with us, Ensign, you focus on organizing, we'll look after the loose bits for you."

The ship was landing as he spoke and they soon stepped down the ramp to be greeted by the Vice-Admiral, the captain of Reacher, and Miriam Holbrooke. "Ebony, what the heck are you up to now?" asked Amanda as she greeted them.

"Not me this time, Vice-Admiral, this one is Brie's baby. I'm just flying backup on this one."

"Stop it, Ebony. You know I need you to organize this."

"Lay it out for me, Brie," smiled Amanda. "Jeannie seems to think this is important."

"Well, ma'am, they got all the people out of that giant bunker and now there are hundreds of prisoners. At least half are women, children, elders, and a few infirm. They're cold, hungry, and terrified; we need to give them food and blankets at least, and we'll need volunteers to help distribute these things."

"I guess I'm on volunteer duty," chuckled Miriam. "How many do you need?"

"At least a dozen," replied Ebony.

"On it," said Miriam as she strode away.

"I'll talk to stores and the kitchen," said Rhonda. "How many food packs and blankets will you need?"

"At least a hundred and fifty," replied Brie, "maybe more."

"Let's go with two hundred, better to have a few extra than not enough." Rhonda was already on her comm as she walked away.

"I assume Chance is organizing the tables etc. that you'll need," said Amanda.

"Already working on it," replied Captain Baris, "and our ship has been designated for transport."

"Very good, however there's one thing you didn't mention, Brie. Medical supplies."

"Oh damn, you're right, we should have some of those too."

"I'll let Carla know you're coming," smiled Amanda.

An hour later Chance Morita had a pile of odd supplies secured in one corner of the ship's hold. As he finished tightening the last strap, the volunteers arrived and the first batch of food packets soon after. Three hours after she landed, Recovery Two was fully loaded with supplies and people. "Now where are our two ...?"

Even as Captain Baris spoke, Ebony and Brie came hurrying along with Dr. Eamon Reilly and two other medics pushing a crate of medical supplies. "Squeeze 'em in, Chance."

"Aye, Captain," chuckled the first officer, as he helped the medics secure their crate. "Everybody grab something and hang on for a quick ride to the surface. We're in luck today, Commander Graves isn't at pilot."

"That's it for you, Chance Morita," grinned Ebony. "I'm taking you along for my next training flight."

"Oh gods, I'm doomed," he groaned.

"Better you than me," giggled Brie.

"Hush you," admonished Ebony, as she lightly poked Brie in the ribs to tickle her.

The ship lifted off then made a swift return to the planet's surface, landing near the makeshift compound the prisoners were being held in. The volunteers spilled out carrying the tables to set up, then came the piles of food packets and stacks of blankets. It was none too soon, as the sun had already gone down and it had grown much colder.

Speaking through the translator, Ebony soon had the women and children lined up for food and blankets. A few were willing to accept medical attention and Dr. Reilly was at the forefront there, always eager to investigate and work with a new species.

Strong light flooded the area, and the security guards were clearly blocking any attempt to flee, but no one really tried. The smell of the food and the sight of blankets drew them closer. Through it all, the Duraden who had flown with Morthel watched silently.

Jeannie and Morthel approached at one point. "Tell me, Garanan," smiled Jeannie, "what do you see?"

"I see lies revealed, great Admiral. I see a weak and confused people who controlled the power to destroy my own, and have done so many times in the past, according to the lore as passed down to me. I see them now cowering in fear, the lie of their power exposed; the truth of their evil clear for all to see.

"Tell me, Admiral. What do you see, and why did you not just destroy your enemy?"

"Walk with me, Garanan, you too, Dour." Jeannie led them over to where Ebony and Brie were working with the women and children. She stopped and pointed to a woman with a small child in her arms, busy trying to wrap the new blanket around herself and the child to warm themselves. "Is this child my enemy? Is its mother? No, I don't believe so. Come."

She led them further around the makeshift compound to where the males of the Paraka were being held separately. Here she pointed out one in a fancy uniform. "Is that man my enemy? Yes, there is no doubt he is. Should I kill him? I don't know as yet, but if I decide to do so he will face me in combat, not be shot by another from a distance.

"My friends, these people are here for many of the same reasons you are, you were all born on this world. Long ago, on their home world, one of them rose to hold power over them all. It was his army who found your ancestors and destroyed them. All those people are long since gone, that once mighty leader is long since dead.

"Sadly, his laws and doctrine live on, and it is those adherents to that doctrine who have plagued you for centuries. They have forced you to be their slaves by pretending to be gods and using their superior technology to make you do their bidding. It is also a sadness that they believe themselves right to do so.

"When I was quite young, I was infected with a disease that killed most of my people. Those few of us who survived it were enslaved by others using superior technology to force us to do their bidding. Eventually I escaped those humans, made peace with most of them, and now we live in harmony, working together. I tell you this to help you understand what I want to do here."

"What is your plan for us, Great Admiral?" asked Dour.

"What I would like to see here, Dour, is a way for all to work together for mutual benefit. Now that we've exposed the Paraka for what they are, I assume the Duraden will no longer hunt or provide food for them."

"You are quite correct there, Admiral. I have sent my last kill to them while I see my own clan go hungry."

"I understand. However, these people have something that would be of great value to you. They have technology, and small shuttle ships which could be used to carry you to the lost worlds and back, keep you in contact with the rest of the Duraden people.

"What I would like to do is to bring the leaders of all the Duraden clans, from all the four worlds, together, to speak to them of these things, and to learn what they would like to see happen. Once the

Duraden are agreed, then we turn our attention to the Paraka, learn what they will need to survive and thrive."

Suddenly Garanan gasped then nodded. "Yes, Great Admiral, I see it now. The ancestors tried to share the knowledge of working together for common benefit but were destroyed. Now the destroyers must admit the rightness of the ancestor's way if they wish to survive.

"Consider this, Dour. Even as the admiral and her SUVI people have helped the humans who once suppressed them, to survive, we can now do the same for the Paraka."

Dour's face became stone as he met Garanan's gaze. "If I find the one among them who released the gray plague upon our clan when I was a boy, I <u>will</u> help him to the afterlife."

Garanan reached out and placed a comforting hand on Dour's shoulder. "Agreed, my friend. Some crimes must not go unanswered. But wisdom requires us to look beyond revenge. Can you support this?" Dour paused considering her words, then nodded solemnly. Garanan turned back toward Suvi-Jean.

" Admiral, what of those who commanded us as gods? I can easily see that the woman with a babe in her arms was not the one to blame, nor is the child, but what of the leaders who are at fault? What did you do about them when you set your own people free?"

"You're right, Garanan, their leaders and those who blindly support them must be removed from the rest. When the SUVI were freed, we sent those who were to blame to a world from which they could not escape, a world where they had no one to serve them, a place where they would live or die by their own efforts."

"Can we do that here?"

"We can. I can have Captain Morthel seek out a place on this world where we could put them, a place from which they could not escape for many generations. This will give your people time to recover and grow strong."

"We are already stronger, thanks to you, Admiral. Now we know and understand what has happened in the past, and we have learned what the ancestors did not know."

"Oh?"

"The ancestors blindly trusted the newcomers, but trust should be earned. Knowledge must be shared, but it must flow both ways, and in the past it did not. SUVI 13 had it easily within his power to kill Dour and his party, but instead he offered friendship and shared a kill. When he was attacked by a foolish boy, he forgave him, and befriended him. This is the way to earn trust."

Jeannie chuckled at that. "Yes, Thirteen is a good man and a great teacher, but he can be tough."

"Yes, as we quickly learned," chuckled Dour, "yet he offered hunter/brother status to me. I have learned much from him. Yes, I like your plan, Admiral. What can we do to help?"

"In the days to come I will need you both to speak to the other clans, and the clans of the lost worlds. Moreover, I will need you to be with me as I try to bring the Paraka in line with the plan. They need to face you when they speak, no longer hiding behind the shield of technology. Will you do this?"

"Yes, Admiral," replied Garanan. "We will do all in our power to help you."

"Thank you both, this truly pleases me. Return to EX2 and get some rest. Tomorrow will prove to be a busy day."

Tearing Down the Old

The night wore on, the guards around the compound were changed, other crews went to their rest, but Jeannie remained, with Sessas by her side. Neither would rest until the Strikers returned.

The first look inside the huge bunker went to Billy as the commander of the Strikers. He encountered no resistance and waved the others inside. "Looks like we got them all."

"No we didn't," replied SUVI 20. "There are a few left; I can feel them."

"Where?"

"Not close, but deeper in." She reached for her comm. "Twenty to Kumar."

"Here."

"I believe there might be a few more still in here. Make another sensor sweep. If you miss any we'll find them and drag them out."

"Working," he chuckled. The sensor sweep turned up two more children who were summarily transported to the compound.

"Kumar to Twenty."

"Here."

"We found two more. Is that all? Sensors read clear."

"There's more. We'll deal with it."

"Twenty, those were kids. You probably will find frightened children hiding somewhere."

"Understood."

As she spoke they had advanced to a small room filled with what looked like control panels. Rayla pulled out an instrument given to her by Linsey da Silva. "Any of it make any sense?" asked Billy.

"Negative. Let me check the sign over the door." She stepped out of the room and waved the instrument over the badly faded sign. "Near as I can tell, this is the control room for the main gate which is no more."

"Understood. Everybody out." As they fled the room, Billy tossed a grenade over his shoulder. The explosion effectively destroyed everything in the room. "Next." Twenty grinned as she led off toward what looked like a weapon emplacement.

Slowly, cautiously, they made their way through the massive underground complex. Outside, the respective first officers had convinced Jeannie and Sessas to get some rest. The sun arose as the Strikers returned, herding three frightened children before them. Jeannie and Sessas were informed and hurried to meet them.

Billy motioned for the strikers to deposit the children with the others in the compound, then approached the admiral. "Billee, report."

"Aye, Captain, Admiral. We did our best to destroy any weapons, or things that could be used to create weapons, we destroyed their transporters, and what looked like a spare parts dump. Everything looked to be in hard shape, like they'd lost the understanding of how some of it actually works, more was just rusting away. There were three shuttles like the one they used to escape us on Planet Two."

"Did you find the gas release controls?"

"We did, Admiral. That one didn't lie; they'd released all of it; at least they'd thrown the switches. There was also a recording of a comm message sent out to all other outposts to release the gas."

"That's disturbing," sighed Jeannie, reaching for her comm. "Eamon, you awake?"

"Here, Jeannie. What's up?"

"The Strikers found evidence that all the gas was released here as well as on the other three planets. Better make sure you have lots of that antidote ready. We're likely to find a disaster on the other three worlds."

"All right, I'll transport back to Reacher and get busy."

"Understood. Sorenson to Vice-Admiral Drake."

"Here, Jeannie."

"Sessas' crew discovered the Paraka probably have released all the gas on every planet in the system. Eamon's on his way to the Reacher to start work on medical supplies for the relief effort."

"I'll make sure he has whatever he needs. Drake out."

Jeannie sighed and reached for SUVI 20's Warhammer. She had painted the head to look like a striking dragon. "Looks like you put a few scratches on her," she grinned.

"Yeah, I've got a few touch ups to do all right. Had fun, though."

"Stress relief?" asked Jeannie, as she passed the weapon back.

"You know it," grinned Twenty, as she hung it back on her belt. "Jeannie, what are we going to do with all these people?"

"I'm working on that right now, but I'll admit it's a work in progress. First, I need Morthel."

"Right behind you, Admiral," came the cheerful voice.

"Morthel, take Garanan and Dour, find all the Duraden clans you can, let them speak, then return with as many of their leaders as you can. I want them all to see what happens here, get their input on any final decisions we make."

Morthel saluted and turned back toward her ship. "On my way, Admiral."

"It'll take them a day or two to get back, give us time to formulate a plan. The biggest concern now will be the plague released on the other planets. They don't have the medicines yet, nor do we have ambassadors to those worlds."

"Maybe we do, Admiral," said Twenty. "Morthel took two prisoners on Planet two, they're still on Reacher. We could go pick them up, outfit them with the same messages etc. that Garanan and Dour have, then send them out with Eamon and his medics."

"I like it, Twenty. You and Sessas make that happen for me. We've got to save as many of these people as we can. Once we're done here, I'll join you and we'll root out the rest of these Paraka and deal with them."

"Aye, Admiral. Come Tentee, we go."

"Yes, ma'am," replied Twenty as she winked at Jeannie then followed Sessas back to the ship. In a few minutes Retriever lifted off and streaked toward Reacher.

"Sorenson to Reacher."

"Rhonda here, Admiral."

"We've captured the compound and the Retriever's savages have had their way with the place. There are three shuttles in there and who knows what else. Send Moira down with Olga's crew to take a look at what's left."

"Understood, Admiral."

* * * * *

Once aboard the Reacher, SUVI 20 explained their mission to the Vice-Admiral. Amanda nodded then called for Linsey da Silva.

"What's up?" asked Linsey as she joined them at the hangar bay.

"Linsey, the Paraka may have released that plague toxin on all four planets. "Eamon will be working on Planet One first, Sessas and Twenty are taking Ordain and Ornan to Planet Two to contact the clans there. Carla will probably go with them to oversee that situation."

"So you want me to check out the folks on Planet Three? Some of them already know about us, shouldn't be a problem. Eighteen is a medic now, if there's a need she can get things started there."

"Do it, Linsey, but be careful. Some of these people may prove hostile, believing that if they kill one of you the gods will spare them."

"Understood. I'll be careful."

"See Carla, take an extra medic with you as well as plenty of vaccine."

"Yes, ma'am. On it," sang Linsey as she hurried away.

"Drake to Orca."

"Sheila here, Vice-Admiral."

"I know the Orca is a war ship, Sheila, but right now I need her to be a medic relief ship. Transport me over and I'll fill you in."

"Understood."

A moment later Amanda disappeared from the Reacher and appeared on the Orca. Captain Singh was waiting for her in the transport area. "Welcome, Vice-Admiral."

"Thank you, Captain Singh. Any chances for a mug of tea and a conference with you and your Chief of Medical?"

"Tea is already waiting in the captain's mess," smiled Sheila, as she reached for her comm to call her Chief of Medical, Commander Harry Erdo. He hurried to the captain's mess to join them.

Amanda took a long sip of her tea then sighed. "It's like this, the Paraka have apparently released all the toxic gas on Planet One."

"Yes, but we've all been inoculated against that, haven't we?" asked Sheila.

"We have," replied Amanda, "and we've inoculated many of the Duraden on Planet One. The thing is, we believe they've done the same on all four planets."

"Well that's not good. I assume you have a plan, how do we fit in?"

"Jeannie has EX2 visiting all the clans of the Duraden on Planet One, explaining to them what has happened and offering medical aid. Retriever is going to Planet Two with the same message, Friendship is on her way to Planet Three ..."

"And we get Planet Four," nodded Sheila. "What do we need to do?"

"You were there for those interviews with the captain of the Paraka ship. Take a copy of that to show them. Dr. Reilly has half the Reacher busy with serum production. Contact him to get your supplies.

"Sheila, be careful with these people. They don't really know us and may think killing one of your crew will buy them forgiveness from their gods."

"Understood. How much time have we got to prepare?"

"None. That gas was released early yesterday."

"Harry."

"I'm already gone, Captain." He was headed for the door, calling Dr. Reilly as he went.

"Captain to Chief of Security."

"Here, Captain."

"Ellen, come to the Captain's mess, the Vice-Admiral has a job for us. It'll be your baby."

"On my way."

Ellen Brady soon arrived and joined them. Amanda laid it out for her, and she nodded. "I'll lead the ground forces myself. I expect Harry will have SUVI 4 with him; I'll take Nineteen with me so there's at least two of them on the ground at the same time."

"Good thinking," chuckled Amanda. "Remember, the idea is to protect the medics without harming the Duraden."

"Understood, Vice-Admiral. I'll go organize a ground crew while Harry's gathering supplies."

"Okay, I've had my break and you've got this well in hand, I guess it's time to return to Reacher and relieve Rhonda."

"Relieve Rhonda?"

"Can't take a baby into a battle zone, so I've been babysitting Twenty-One. Man, that little girl has a strong grip, darn near broke my finger. Anyway, I handed her off to Rhonda when I went to meet the incoming ships. She should have the diaper changed by now."

Sheila laughed heartily at that. "Amanda Drake, you're a bad woman."

"And proud of it," chuckled Amanda, as she set aside her empty cup and rose from the chair.

* * * * *

While Amanda retrieved Twenty-One from Captain Moore, the child's parents watched carefully while Garanan spoke with the chieftain and lore speaker of another clan. The confusion and fear on the faces of the new clan was easy to read. Thirteen's keen hearing could make out the coughing from the hidden cave.

Slowly the new clan began to fall into despair as they realized they had been deceived and that the gods could not help them against the disease. Their leaders consented to the medicines and agreed to accompany EX2 back to confront the Paraka. They boarded the ship with Garanan and EX2 set out to find the next clan.

Back at the compound, Jeannie was cursing as she gazed at the storm clouds gathering on the horizon. "Dammit, this is going to complicate things. All right, grab any Paraka in a fancy uniform and transport them to the brig on the Reacher... oh wait, Mandy filled Reacher's brig... we'd better lock them in Recovery Two's cargo hold until Orca gets back, then we can send them to her brig if we need to. Tell Nine to choose a partner to help him on guard duty on Recovery Two. Get the rest back inside the caverns. Move the makeshift kitchens inside as well.

"Hal, make sure you have sufficient security, and be careful. Keep an eye out for Ebony and Brie's crew as well."

"I got this, Jeannie. You haven't slept in two days; go home and get some rest. That storm will keep things quiet here and it'll take Morthel a few days to complete her mission."

She gave him a friendly pat on the shoulder then called for transport back to the Reacher, leaving the crew of F1 behind to back up Hal should he need them. Amanda met her in the transportation arrivals area and gave her a full report.

"You're amazing, my super organized and bewitchingly beautiful companion. You make my job so much easier."

"God, you suck up nice," chuckled Amanda, as she took Jeannie by the arm and led her toward their quarters. "Come on, love. I'll take you home and tuck you in."

"Works for me. Mandy, if the whole fleet is on mercy missions, who is watching our backs?"

"Rhonda, she has the best long-range weapon, plus Probie is well out watching for anything at all suspicious. Relax and rest, my darling SUVI, we've got it all under control." Amanda stopped to open the door to their quarters then led Jeannie inside.

* * * * *

Ebony and Brie sank into the seats of Recovery Two. "Are you sure about this? Shouldn't we be out there helping?"

"Nope," replied Ebony. "Honey, the key here is, all these folks are super capable people, that's why they were chosen for the colonizing efforts in the first place. They know what needs to be done and how to do it. Security will see to their safety, and now we show them that we have full confidence in them by backing off to let them do the job we asked them to do."

"Build up flagging confidence?"

"Yep."

"Did you do that to me?"

"What? Brie, no, geez, don't be silly. Woman, I've been besotted with you since the first time I saw you. Heck, I'll even confess I was showing off a bit the day we captured that robot just to impress you."

"Impress me, you nearly killed me, gods. Ebony, do you really mean that?"

"Yeah, I do. I've been looking for a way to tell you, but life always seems to get in the way. When you came up with this idea I was truly sunk, not only the girl of my dreams, but she thinks like me too. Tell me I've actually got a chance here."

Brie slid over and snuggled into Ebony's arms. "Your chances are better than average," she giggled. "I was whining to Edran about how I wanted to get closer with you and they suggested I find a project like you do, one that helps everybody, especially the passengers.

"When I saw that woman shivering as she tried to keep her baby warm, I knew I had the right project, and it looked like the Admiral was focused elsewhere. Everybody was waiting for her to give the orders, so if it was going to happen someone would have to bring it to her attention."

"Oh yeah? So, you set me up?"

"Sure did. What are you going to do about it?"

"How about I show you," breathed Ebony, as she pulled Brie closer and kissed her. She moaned with delight and arousal as Brie deepened the kiss and slipped her long elegant fingers into Ebony's uniform.

"Oh gods, Ebony, I dare you to do that again," gasped Brie, as their lips slowly parted. Ebony was more than happy to oblige.

"Take that back to the sleeping quarters, ladies," grinned Chance Morita, as he entered the ship. "Don't want to distract the security forces, now do we?"

"Darn fine idea, Commander," grinned Ebony, as she stood and offered her hand to Brie. Wide-eyed, Brie accepted the hand and allowed herself to be led back to the small sleeping quarters. Chance grinned to himself as he settled into the pilot's chair and pulled on the headset, blocking out all sounds from within the ship.

A Workable Solution

It was two days later when EX2 returned with a full load of Duraden lorespeakers, ready to face the gods and see the truth of the matter for themselves. The sun was bright overhead when the Paraka were all marched outside to face them.

Jeannie, using the loudspeakers, greeted the Duraden representatives, then explained what was going to happen. She called for the Paraka leaders to be escorted from Recovery Two's hold so they could face the people they had subjugated for so long. In moments they began to arrive and were marched a short distance aside. A moment later, inhabitants of Reacher's brig were transported to an area a short distance from the other two groups. As soon as they had them all, she spoke again.

"We're all here, let us now begin. Long ago, the Paraka attacked and defeated the people of this world and destroyed as much of their way of life as they could. They did this on the orders of their supreme commander, the One.

"Once the Duraden were defeated, the Paraka demanded regular tribute from them in the form of food. As time went on they began to call themselves the gods, and if the Duraden refused to obey their commands, they released a deadly disease upon them. That has now stopped forever, for we have found and destroyed that gas.

"We have also exposed the Paraka parasites for what they are. They will now face the Duraden for these crimes. Who speaks for the Duraden?"

"We do," replied Garanan as she and the other lorespeakers stepped forward.

"Thank you, lorespeakers. Who speaks for the Paraka?" No one moved. Jeannie sighed and motioned for Hal to bring the Paraka leaders forward. She stepped up to one and went nose to nose with him. "Who was in command of the garrison in that bunker?" He didn't respond so she stepped back and shot him. He fell to the ground twitching.

She stepped to the next. "Who was in command of that garrison?" Same result, same response.

As the second man fell the next in line began to babble. "Him," he stammered, "that man, he is the One."

"The One as in the commander, or the One as in the supreme leader?"

"Both. He speaks for the One here and commands everything." There were groans from the two fallen men as the effects of the stunner began to wear off. The man who had spoken turned, startled to see his companions revive.

"It was set on light stun," grinned Jeannie. She pointed at the man who had been the commander. "Bring him." SUVI 13 grabbed the hapless man and shoved him along behind Jeannie.

She walked a short way apart to make sure there was room, then turned to the man. "Several times you have commanded my death. Now is your big chance to see it done." She tossed aside her stunner and spread her arms wide. "Come, show us your god power and strike me down."

"Kill her, kill her now," he bellowed, and over a dozen Paraka surged forward, but were brought down by the security forces. That drew her attention for only a split second, but he seized the opportunity and swept up the weapon.

Jeannie easily batted it aside then slowly advanced toward the man who stood glaring at her. "Stop wasting time and do it," he snarled as he stepped back from her. "Kill me and have done."

With a shake of her head, she walked away, returning to the gathering. "Bring him." The man was hauled back and stood before the Duraden. "You will now answer to the voices of the Duraden, they will decide the fate of your people. Garanan."

Looking regal as she straightened up to her full height and advancing on the man, she spoke. "The Lore speakers have asked me to speak for all. Is this acceptable to you, Great Admiral?"

"The lore speakers have chosen wisely. Proceed, Garanan."

Garanan advanced on the cowering man. "I am old now, as are you, but you appear to be older. In the days of my youth, the gray plague came to my people, and many other clans as well. Did you give the order for that to be released against us?"

She received no response. "Admiral?"

"Use whatever means necessary to elicit a response, Garanan."

"May I borrow your weapon?"

"Of course," chuckled Jeannie as she passed the stunner to Garanan. She leaned close to the Paraka. "That weapon won't kill you, but the pain, I cannot begin to describe the pain."

With a whimper of fear, he answered the question. "Yes. The gas was released only once in my lifetime. There was a clan that refused to share the meat, I had no choice but to punish them."

"There were several years of hunger, our clan was starving. Every kill, every grain gathered was needed ..." Garanan fairly trembled as she fought to keep from killing the man where he stood. "Great Admiral, the hate I and all Duraden bear for these people is too great. We beg you, do not leave their fate in our hands, for if you do, they will all perish where they stand.

"You are great in wisdom, Admiral. Please share with us your wisdom, what do you suggest we do here?"

Jeannie nodded then looked around. "Ebony, Brie, bring me those two." She was pointing at a female Paraka with a small child in her arms."

Ebony took the terrified woman by the arm. "Relax, the admiral won't hurt you or the child. It'll be okay, I promise." The woman swallowed hard then went with them.

As they reached Jeannie, she smiled and reached out to stroke the child's cheek. "Look at them, Garanan, this woman is not your enemy, nor is the child. She gave no order to harm you, but that one surely did."

Garanan sighed and gazed at the woman who met her gaze but held the child away protectively. "I understand, great Admiral. These people are not the enemy, their leaders are. If we no longer share food with them this woman and her child will starve. May I speak with the others for a moment?" At Jeannie's nod she turned to the other lore speakers.

"The admiral is right, my sisters. While I was on the great sky ship called Reacher, home to the admiral and her people, I saw many things of wonder. I saw many different people working together in harmony. Indeed, there among the varied species are those like the Paraka, those who enslaved the admiral's own people."

"Why tell us this, Garanan?" asked the youngest of the lore speakers.

"The admiral forgave those people and now has become their commander. I was told she put the leaders of those people on a place where they could do no harm and left them there. She then took the rest of them aboard the great sky ship to become her own people."

"Are you saying we should do the same?"

"Look for yourself; that young mother and child brought no harm to the Duraden. They will die of starvation if we don't help them. Could you put the spear to the child's heart?"

With a sigh, she replied. "No, I couldn't, for my own son is about the same age. You are wise, Garanan. I believe we should do as you say." There was a round of agreement from the others. Garanan turned back to Jeannie.

"Great Admiral, we have agreed on the fate of these people. We would ask your help to make this happen."

"We will help you, Garanan. What is the decision of the Duraden?"

The entire field of captives held their breath as Garanan turned to face them. "We would have these people removed to a more accessible place where the Duraden can teach them to hunt and harvest for themselves. Destroy all their machines and leave their leaders here to fend for themselves.

"Here me, Paraka people. We will help you learn to survive, we will trade fairly with you, but we will never again be your servants. Never again will we obey your commands without question. We will face the future with you as equals. The alternative is to leave you here to starve in these barren mountains."

Jeannie smiled as she nodded and turned to face the Paraka. "You have heard the decision of the Duraden. What say you, will you go with them and learn how to survive, or will you remain here to fend for yourselves?"

To everyone's surprise the woman with the child stepped up to Garanan and spoke. "I have never harmed you, any of you, and knew nothing of a plague, and yet I have had a safe life because of your efforts. It is now time to repay some of that debt. I and my child will go with you, learn what you teach."

Garanan looked her over for a long moment then nodded. "What is your name?"

"I am Talala and this is Carn."

"I will do what I can to help you, Talala. We will not harm you or the child. Great Admiral, how do we go about this?"

"My people will take care of the relocation, Garanan. Hal, put the leaders and any who obeyed his order to attack me back in the compound." That was quickly accomplished. When Hal gave her the signal, Jeannie spoke to the Paraka.

"Hear me, Paraka people, those of you who would go with the Duraden and learn how to survive, stay where you are. Those who wish to remain with your leaders, go back inside the bunker." She turned and spoke quietly to Sessas. "Your strikers did destroy all the tech, right?"

"Tentee take Warhammer, tech destroyed."

"You're right of course. Whatever was I thinking?" She smiled at Sessas's hissing laughter.

As they waited, barely a quarter of the Paraka returned to the bunker and disappeared inside. Jeannie sighed as she watched. When it was finished, she turned to the captain of EX2. "Morthel, take your Duraden friends and locate a new home for these fine folks. Meanwhile we'll ferry them up to the Reacher."

Morthel saluted and trotted back toward her ship, calling for her crew as she went. As soon as she had everyone on board, the ship lifted off. Soon after that, the Paraka were ferried to Reacher in the two Recovery ships, then housed in passenger quarters with security guards posted. Recovery Two returned and gathered up the remaining supplies and accessories left on the planet.

By nightfall those Paraka left behind at the bunker were back outside, searching the grounds for any scraps of food that had been overlooked by the ship's crews.

The next day Jeannie got a call from Morthel, the Duraden had chosen a site and wanted her to see it. She boarded F1 and set out for the provided coordinates.

The site was at the edge of the great city, near a small stream for water, and easy access to the grain fields. "This place is a bit too open," said Garanan, "but there is water and grain. Gleaning is easier than hunting. The Bi-Lad will relocate here as well to help them learn to hunt. There is shelter among the buildings.

"We considered this move once before, but we were too few to hold it against the predators. With so many here it will be easier, and many more guards can be posted."

"So, you're happy with this arrangement?"

"This will test us for certain, Great Admiral. However, we will teach them what we can, and learn as much from them as possible. The Te-Jak clan will also move to this area to help. There is a fine spot not far from here. The Ne-Lod are also considering a move here to help. Together we will all prosper."

"So you plan to use the forbidden knowledge of your people to help these folks?"

Garanan smiled at that. "Yes, we will teach them the proper way."

"Well then, if you're ready, we'll bring them down. We'll also provide enough food packets and a few simple tools to make things a bit easier for you to get started. Sorenson to Commander Graves."

"Ebony here, Admiral."

"All yours, Ebony, send them down."

"Aye, Admiral. Operation relocation underway."

Garanan quirked an eyebrow at Jeannie, who smiled. "This is Ebony's idea. She and her partner arranged to have the prisoners fed and given blankets back at the bunker. Now they've arranged for a number of former colonists to come down with simple tools and such to help. Those people have experience in setting up a new colony."

"We will be grateful for any and all the knowledge they are willing to share, Admiral."

Jeannie waited until the Paraka had landed and the ship load of supplies and former colonists arrived. She introduced them to Garanan, then left them all to it. The two recovery ships were assigned to the project as well. When she was sure they had everything in hand, she took F1 and returned to Reacher. Amanda met her at the landing bay.

"Mandy, report, what's happening on the rest of the system?"

"Morthel has gone back to Planet Two, spreading the medicines and hunting for Paraka. She's got her Duraden guide with her, so that looks good. Sessas is on Planet Three spreading the medicine and the message. In truth, I think she's a bit miffed that there are no Paraka there to find since it was that group that fled to the bunker on Planet One.

"Sheila is working on Planet Four. They've got a real mess on their hands there. The plague was well established when she located the Duraden, and those people seemed determined to kill a human to win the favor of the gods, to lift the plague. She says it's a work in progress.

"From what I can piece together, and from what Marcus managed to get from the prisoners when we had them here, it appears that the main bunker on Planet One was the stronghold, the installations on the other planets seem to be only outposts with a small number of soldiers."

"And what about open space?"

"Probie and Rhonda both report clear skies. All we can do now is wait until our people finish mopping this up."

"Okay, sounds good. Take me to Simple Pleasures and then take me home and make me forget my troubles."

"It will be my pleasure to do so, my beloved companion. Amanda to Maxi."

"Maxi here. Did you finally get the admiral to come home?"

"She's here and anxious to try all the new treasures."

"I'll have a table loaded when you get here. Maxi out."

Jeannie sighed with delight as she sampled the new cake Alli had developed. "So, everything is good here?" asked the tall blonde, as she appeared at their table.

"Better than, Maxi," replied Jeannie. "Tell me, are Ebony and Brie next door in the studio?"

"Yes," chuckled Maxi. "I just took over a round of seconds for them."

"Ask them to join us for a moment, will you please?"

"Yes, ma'am, be right back." She sped away then soon returned with Ebony and Brie.

"You wanted to see us, Admiral?"

"Yes, please join us." As soon as they were seated, she spoke again. "I've been keeping an eye on you two ever since you caught that oversight on Planet One. You took control of the problem and, better still, you managed to pull a number of our former colonists in to help you. That had a double benefit in that it got the job done without undue strain on ship's crews.

"Miriam tells me you do this a lot."

"Not just the colonists, Admiral," replied Ebony, "but sky-riders too. There's lots of folks who have no real job or hate the one they have. We try to find ways for them to fit in and enjoy what they do."

"Like Maxi there, and Alli."

"Yes, like that. The colonists were eager to help those folks, since they'd been in a similar situation on Elysium. Dozens volunteered to help the Paraka resettle."

"And you liaise with Miriam and Social Engagement to find the right people?"

"Yes, and Antha."

"Antha, the ship's councilor?"

"Yes, she can often point us to someone who needs help and will be a good fit for something we've got in the works."

Brie sighed and spoke. "Actually, Admiral, this stuff is all Ebony. Down on the planet was my first crack at trying anything like this, and I bullied Ebony into bringing it to you. She should get the credit for the success."

Jeannie smiled at her. "So you saw a need, devised a way to meet that need, then began to recruit the people most likely to succeed in getting the job done, is that right?"

"Uh, yeah, I guess."

"Grandfather gave a rather glowing report of how you handled the project, Brie. You did good and I thank you for it, both of you. Tell me you plan to keep doing things like this."

"Oh yeah," chuckled Ebony, "we will. It's fun really, watching it come together, seeing folks suddenly come alive as they find themselves making a difference, feeling useful for a change. Maxi, for example, lost and bored to death working in stores, counting stuff. She's a people person. Look how much she enjoys the people here, talking to them, bringing them treats, making them smile."

"I had noticed that, Ebony. The reason I called you out here was to thank you both for all your efforts in this current situation. I also wanted to tell you not to be shy about approaching me or Amanda if you have a project on the go that needs a bit of a push to get it moving.

"What you're doing is every bit as important to our eventual survival as any other. Yes, we need engineers, botanists, medics, warriors, and more, but all that is just to protect and provide for a happy and growing populace. In my job, I have to focus on our survival; I have far too little time for the happy thriving part. I'm thrilled to see you taking that on, and I'll support your efforts whenever I can."

"Wow," said Brie, "thank you, Admiral. I don't know what to say."

"Say you'll keep it up."

"Keep it up? Ma'am, we're just getting started, right Ebony?"

"Absolutely right, my love, now let's leave these folks to their snacks and go see what mischief we can get into. With your permission, Admiral."

"Go play, girls, have fun."

"That was sweet, Jeannie," said Amanda, as they watched the girls disappear out the back.

"Mandy, those two characters have done what I was unable to do; they've just solved our grounders problem. I'll do all I can to help them succeed."

Mopping Up

Jeannie slept late the next day and shook an admonishing finger at Amanda when she found her on the bridge of the Reacher. "Good morning, Admiral, sleep well?" grinned the Vice-Admiral.

"Yes I did and you know it," chuckled Jeannie. "Why didn't you wake me?"

"You've been running on empty for days, rarely eating or taking time to rest. We have the situation under control now, so I let you sleep in. Did you get anything to eat?"

"Not yet, join me in the mess? You can bring me up to speed while I get some breakfast."

"Capital idea, let's go."

When they were settled at the table, Amanda sipped her tea and began her report. "As things stand now, it looks as though we've cleaned out the Paraka from all four planets, thanks to Morthel's engineer cracking their sensor blocks. Those found by Sheila and Sessas were just as you suspected, small garrisons, outposts manned by fighters only, no families.

"Each captain gave the captives a choice, return to the leaders at the bunker or join the families with the Duraden."

"How did that work out?"

"Most went to the bunker, but a few with young families joined the colony."

"Good. So, are Sessas and Sheila back?"

"Yes, Retriever is aboard Reacher and the Orca is back on patrol."

"I know EX2 and the Recovery ships are helping the colony now, but I'd like to have a full captain's meeting."

"Bring in Miriam too?"

"Absolutely."

"All right, finish your tea while I go arrange it. 1300 hrs?"

"Works for me, Mandy." Amanda patted her shoulder and walked away, already on comms organizing the meeting. Jeannie took the opportunity to relax with a second mug of Earalithian tea.

* * * * *

While Amanda was taking Jeannie for breakfast, Morthel and Thirteen were watching Brodie explain something to Ravel. "What do you think, Thirteen?"

"I think we're about to lose an engineer or gain a hunter/ engineering apprentice."

"That is my thought as well. It's only been a few weeks, but Brodie seems to have matured years and gained a handle on the agoraphobia."

"Yes he has, but it's Ravel that helped him get it under control. He, too, has matured since throwing that spear at me. I'm not sure just what happened here, especially between those two."

Morthel laughed at that. "Oh come on, think about it. They were both terrified of you and that gave them something big in common, the bond grew from that. Once they began to understand they both preferred male companionship, the rest was natural."

"Yes, I guess you're right there."

Morthel's comm pinged. "Amanda to Morthel."

"Here, Vice-Admiral."

"There's a meeting of the captains. Leave your ship there if needed, EX4 has been watching the bunker. Hal can swing by and give you a lift or you can transport up."

"I'd prefer the transport; it will give me time for lunch with sweet Antha."

"Transport it is." A moment later Morthel vanished in a flash of light leaving Lilly Peters in command.

* * * * *

"All captains and passenger representatives present, Admiral."

"Thank you, Vice Admiral. All right, let's see if we can wrap this one up. Sheila, what's the situation on Planet Four?"

"The Duraden have been informed of the Paraka hoax, the Paraka outpost has been located and destroyed. The soldiers found there have been dispersed to the bunker and the colony, along with the remaining spacefaring Paraka. We called it done and went back to patrolling."

"Excellent. Sessas?"

"Same, same, Planet Three, all good."

"Morthel?"

"Planet two has been cleared, Admiral. All the action is on Planet One now. The Paraka have been settled somewhat in their new colony with the aid of two Duraden clans plus a large contingent of volunteers from the Reacher."

"Would you say we're ready to let them fly on their own?"

"Soon, I think. Perhaps Miriam might have a better take on this."

"Miriam?"

"Actually, Admiral, the volunteers on the ground would like to stay another month or two to make certain things are going to work out. There's a bit of a problem with big predators and spears are a poor deterrent. They're getting the hang of harvesting and milling the grain that grows everywhere but converting the stalks into fiber for clothing is taking a while to teach.

"We believe they need more time."

"I see."

"I'm with Miriam on this one, Admiral."

"Rhonda?"

"We depleted many of our resources in the hunt for the gods and in their subsequent relocation. Moira wants to pillage that mass of dead robots, and stores would love to harvest more of that grain, top up our food supply. I'm told there are vast areas of it untouched on Planet Four."

Jeannie looked thoughtful for a moment. "Why not, it does make sense. This system is rich in resources and has only a sparse population. A few more weeks will give us time to stock up, teach the Duraden how to operate the shuttles we took from the Paraka, let them stay in touch with all four planets.

"The Duraden on Planet Two seemed to have advanced their weapons beyond simple spears, perhaps they can help the others on Planet One with the predator problem. All right, we'll stick around for a while and do what we can to help the Duraden while we resupply.

"Is there anything further?"

"Just this, Admiral," smiled Miriam. "A number of our former colonists would like to thank you for this opportunity to get their hands dirty again. We realize that a colony isn't in the cards for us right now, but they're enjoying helping the Paraka learn a new way of life."

"Actually, the credit for that goes to Ebony Graves and Brie Elliot. Those two characters engineered much of this effort, and I'll be happy to pass along your message."

Miriam chuckled at that. "Yes, they cornered me in Simple Pleasures and gave me a list of people and skills they needed for volunteers."

"Tell me, Miriam, is this situation doing what I think it's doing?"

"You mean giving the former colonists a feeling of being a part of the Reacher, of the combined peoples of the fleet? Yes, I believe it is. It's bringing them to life, giving them purpose, making them feel as though they have value."

"Then we stay here until the passenger representatives tell us it is safe to leave the Duraden/Paraka colony on its own."

* * * * *

Down on the planet, Brie Elliot grabbed the loudspeaker. "Attention, your attention please. I have important news." She waited a few moments until the gathered people settled down. "Word has come down from the admiral. The fleet will remain here until the volunteers report the new colony of Duraden/Paraka is ready to fly on its own. That is all."

There was a round of cheers from the volunteers. One approached her. "Is this true? Is the fleet really going to wait until we say we can safely leave these folks on their own?"

"Yes. Apparently, when Miriam explained to the admiral that you all felt these folks needed more time, she agreed to wait until you give the all-clear."

"Well I'll be damned," he sighed. "I never would have guessed it; SUVI 5 actually listened to us."

"Well, apparently she did and agreed with you. This project is all yours now," she grinned. "Call me if you need anything." With that she patted his shoulder and walked back to Recovery One.

"He looks happy," said Olga Volkov, as Brie resumed her station.

"These folks have a lot of knowledge, Captain, but they haven't had much chance to use it for a long time, according to Ebony. It must feel good to finally get to do the thing you wanted to in the first place."

"You're right, Brie. I bet it felt good to bring them good news for a change."

"Yeah, they haven't had a lot of that from us. It did feel good."

"Then let's leave them to it and go home for a rest. You can tell Ebony all about it."

"If I can track her down," chuckled Brie.

* * * * *

"Well there goes the ship," said Ravel, as he put his arm around Brodie's shoulders. "How are you doing?"

"I'm a little shaky, but I'll be fine," replied Brodie, leaning against Ravel.

"How did you manage to get permission to come down and stay anyway?"

"I told the captain I wanted to help everybody learn to get comfortable with some basic tech and how to operate the shuttles, what could go wrong with them and how to fix it. I also told her I need the time in the open spaces to beat the agoraphobia. She agreed to let me try it on the condition that I call for help if I need it."

"Think she's figured it out yet?"

"Probably. Captain Morthel is no fool. She knows darn well it will take years to train someone to be a competent pilot and shuttle tech."

"They say the fleet is staying until the volunteer farmers say it's time to go. I could learn to fly one in the next few weeks. You've still got time to change your mind."

"Ah-huh, and if you say anything like that again I'll put a short circuit in the seat to zap your ass every time you sit in the pilot's chair. You said you want me to stay, so now you're stuck with me."

"Then my life is blessed," chuckled Ravel, as he hugged Brodie's shoulders then released him. "So, back to that damned circuit bypass relay ..."

Round Up

All captains were in the briefing room awaiting the admiral's arrival as she and Vice-Admiral Drake breezed in arm in arm. "We're all here, Admiral," said Captain Rhonda Moore.

Jeannie smiled as she and Amanda settled into their seats. "Thank you, Rhonda. Well, people, I'm getting that old itch to go exploring, see what we can find out there. We've been hanging around here for two months now, what say you, are we ready?"

"Recovery ships fit and ready, Admiral."

"Friendship is good to go and ready for the next adventure."

"You always are, Linsey. I like that. Sessas?"

"Retriever crew bored, ship ready to go."

"Orca is ready, Admiral."

The Kreenon stands ready, Admiral."

"EX2 is ready, Admiral, but I believe I'll need a new engineer."

"Oh?"

"It seems that the current engineer has decided to remain behind with the Duraden to help train them in the use and repair of the three shuttlecraft we captured from the Paraka."

"Could not one of the Paraka do that?"

"Perhaps, but I believe Brodie may have another reason to request to stay."

"The tall Duraden lad who tried to assassinate me?"

Morthel laughed at that. "Yes, Admiral, I do believe young Ravel might have something to do with his decision."

"This would be your decision, Captain Morthel."

"Thank you, Admiral. I did express to him that leaving even a single person behind diminishes our small gene pool and weakens us as a species."

"What was his response to that?"

"He paid a visit to Dr. Reilly and left several samples of his DNA for future use."

"Then he is indeed determined. What did you tell him?"

"I left the decision to him, Admiral. I expect he will stay behind when we move on."

"So be it. Hal?"

"EX4 fit and ready, Admiral."

"Good to know. F1 is also ready for the next adventure. So, we're all set to go then?"

"If I may, Admiral, there is an issue from the passengers."

Jeannie let her shoulders sag as she leaned back in her chair. "They want to stay and establish a colony, don't they, Miriam?"

"A few do, yes."

"A few?"

"Ebony's volunteers and a few more want to stay, and they want to know if Reacher will stick around for a few years to make sure they're secure."

Jeannie sighed and seemed lost in thought. No one disturbed her. Finally she brought her attention back to the room. "Morthel, call Lilly Peters here, would you? I want her opinion on this."

Morthel nodded and reached for her comm. "Commander Lilly Peters to the bridge briefing room. Repeat, Commander Lilly Peters to the bridge briefing room."

"On my way, Captain." She arrived a few minutes later.

"Have a seat, Lilly."

"Thank you, Admiral."

"Lilly, give us your assessment of this planet for a colony, any of the four in the Goldilocks Zone for that matter."

"Of course, Admiral. First, let me say, I don't like it. On a scale of one to ten I'd give any of them a five, a six at best."

"Why, Lilly?" asked Miriam, as she leaned forward in her seat to place her elbows on the table. "The atmosphere is good, there's food everywhere, and the local inhabitants have invited us to stay. What's the big problem?"

Everyone was paying close attention now. "I agree that, at first glance, they seem perfect. A second look tells me that long ago they were terra formed by the Duraden to meet their needs. There is little variety of food source, and as Dr. Reilly will tell you, that's a problem for the Duraden themselves and a much bigger one for humans.

"The Earalith could survive longest here, but in the end that small food source would cause malnutrition. Humans would falter in as few as five years. Even the Duraden who are well adapted to this have issues.

"They have only two different food grains, and those lack certain nutrients that they currently get from meat products, but the source is sketchy. Humans would have to introduce a large number of different plants to increase the possibilities."

"But isn't that what you do? Isn't that the overall plan, to add what we need to whatever planet we choose?" asked Miriam.

"Yes, that's the overall idea, but whenever you introduce something new to an ecosystem, the results can be catastrophic for the native flora and fauna. Introduce something prolific that has no predators and even the atmosphere can be affected. On an uninhabited planet, that's not such a big issue.

"However, here we have an inhabited system, four planets that have been drained of certain nutrients in the soil, etc. If we start terraforming one of these planets, we could possibly bring about the end of the Duraden on that planet."

Miriam nodded and sat back, absorbing all Lilly had said. Morthel turned to Lilly. "Have you mentioned any of this to Brodie?"

"Not yet, why, is he planning to stay behind?"

"He is."

"I'll have a chat with him after this meeting, Captain. He needs to have all the information before making that decision."

Jeannie rose and began pacing about. "Miriam, do you want a few days to share this information with your people then get back to me with it?"

"Yes, that would be best, Admiral. Admiral, may I ask what your answer would be if they decide to stay?"

"Miriam, I won't hold the entire fleet back to babysit thirty or forty colonists, nor will I give them the means to introduce new and possibly dangerous species to the Duraden worlds. These are not our worlds, they're occupied. We have no right to claim them for our own or to introduce possibly harmful species.

"If any wish to stay, knowing the possible health issues they may face in future, I won't hinder them, but Dr. Reilly will want to keep their DNA in our gene pool. They will have to agree to this."

Miriam nodded. "More than fair, Admiral. I'll call a general meeting tonight, then go down to the surface and repeat the process for those who are on the ground. I'll have an answer for you in a couple of days."

"Take your time, Miriam, make sure they understand the issues and our position on the matter. Commander Peters, you're from the caverns, as are those volunteers and potential colonists. Go with Miriam to answer any question these folks may have.

"Captain Morthel, EX2 can act as transport for Miriam in this case."

"Of course, Admiral. We're at your disposal, Miriam. Just call me when you need a ride."

"First thing tomorrow?"

"I'll have the ship ready for travel," smiled Morthel.

The meeting broke up then and Miriam hurried away to call a general meeting of the passengers for that evening. There was a lot of disappointment as Lilly explained her objections, but in the end, there was general consensus, they would move on.

The meeting on the ground was even livelier, but when it was over, they gathered their gear and said their goodbyes to the Duraden/ Paraka colony. Miriam called ahead and, as the disappointed volunteers helped to unpack their gear from EX2, Jeannie arrived with Amanda.

"Looks like you're still stuck with us, Admiral," said one man as he set down the pack he was carrying.

"It's okay, I'm starting to like you folks a lot," grinned Jeannie. "I just came down to tell you how proud I am of how you all pitched in to help those people, and I won't hesitate to call on you again if the need arises."

The big man chuckled at that. "We're always glad to help, Admiral. It's good to feel useful once in a while."

"Yes, well, next time the boredom gets the better of you, check in with Ebony Graves, she might be able to help."

"Seriously?"

"Seriously."

"All right," he nodded, "I'll do just that. Thanks." With that he gathered up his pack and walked away.

Jeannie turned to Morthel. "Can we get a lift down to the surface? I want to say goodbye to Garanan and wish her well."

"Pleasure, Admiral," smiled Morthel.

Garanan came to greet them as the ship landed. "Greetings, Garanan, I'm told you have been chosen as leader for this new colony. Congratulations."

"Thank you, Admiral. Have you come to say goodbye?"

"I have, that and to wish you and your combined people well. I don't know if we'll ever come back this way, so this is farewell."

"May you and your people walk in wisdom, great Admiral. You have our undying gratitude for all you have done here. The lore of your visit and generosity will be sung forever by the lore speakers who follow me."

"The finding and the friendship of the Duraden is logged and will be long remembered with fondness. Be well, Garanan." With that she and Amanda returned to the ship. Thirteen was there saying farewell to Dour, Ravel, and Brodie.

As EX2 lifted off and disappeared into the sky Ravel put an arm around Brodie. "There they go. You can still call."

"Nope, I'm good right here."

"What was in that crate they left for you?"

"A lifetime supply of vitamins and minerals."

"And those are?"

"Nutrients I can't get in the food here. Can we get back inside out of all this open space now?"

"Yes we can," chuckled Ravel, as he gently hugged Brodie then led him back inside the building they were making into a home.

Later that evening they stood outside and watched the sky as three points of light winked out. The fleet had gone exploring.

And now for a peek at the next adventure in the Forgotten Worlds series.

IGEN

by

Prudence MacLeod

A Puzzle

"Floo, are you certain?"

"I am, Eelee, see here? It's outside Igen right now."

"Are you sure, I see only a flashing point of light darting about."

"That's how this is supposed to work, Eelee, the flashing light speaks of an object outside Igen. See how fast it moves, and changes direction to stay close? The original purpose of Igen has been served, the great question answered, they do exist, and we have been found."

"Floo, what can we do?"

"Pray they can't find a way in, or that the Gants don't let them in."

"And if they do?"

"Kill them before they kill us." Slowly she nodded her head in agreement, he was right she knew, he always was. "We need to get out of here, I hear the Gants coming. We don't want to be caught in the open light." Together they sprinted away.

* * * * *

Admiral Jeannie Sorenson stood on the bridge of the Reacher, the last home of humanity and a few other species. The admiral was one of only twenty SUVI, a species of mutated humans, and at this point her agile mind was completely intrigued. "Sorenson to EX2, report."

Her call was answered by the captain of the explorer ship EX2, a woman of the Earalith, one of only a dozen still in existence. "Morthel here, Admiral. It's definitely a ship, extremely old, moving under the momentum gained sometime in the past. There are hundreds, perhaps thousands, of life signs on board, but Thirteen believes them to be feral."

"Feral?"

"Their movements are more like hunting or grazing animals, no stationary activity on what we believe to be the bridge, or near the main power source, nor anywhere near the main engines which have gone cold."

"Gone cold?"

"We believe it was originally nuclear powered, Admiral. It has another power source maintaining atmosphere and some other vital systems."

"Any response to hails?"

"None, Admiral."

"Docking ports?"

"We found several, all locked tight."

"Come home, Morthel. We need to put our heads together."

"Aye, Admiral, coming home." With that the agile explorer ship turned and shot away from the massive object and back toward the Reacher.

* * * * *

As usual, Admiral Sorenson was pacing while the others assembled in the Reacher's briefing room. Finally, everyone arrived and settled into a chair. "All ships captains and passenger representatives present, Admiral."

"Thank you, Vice Admiral Drake." Jeannie smiled then took her seat at the head of the table. "All right, people, we have a bit of a puzzle on our hands. Five days ago the Maccay observers on the Kreenon picked something up on sensors about halfway between systems. By the time we realized it was artificial and got the fleet stopped, we'd overshot it by a couple of days.

"We backtracked and located the object then EX2 went out for a look. Captain Morthel, report."

"The object is a ship, Admiral," replied Morthel. "It's roughly the size of the Reacher, traveling mainly on momentum gained sometime in the past. Its main nuclear engines are cold, but it has a secondary power source still functioning. There are a large number of life signs aboard, but we believe them to be feral. We tried hailing them with every language in Linsey's database but received no answer."

"Feral? How did you reach that conclusion?" asked Miriam Holbrooke, President of the Passengers Association.

"SUVI Thirteen came to that conclusion after observing the movements of the life signs," replied Morthel. "A working ship will have a number of stationary life signs, people working at stations like sensors, etc. We found no such stationary signs. Instead, what we could see looked to Thirteen like herds of animals and hunters stalking them."

"I see, that does make sense, and he would understand what he was seeing."

Jeannie chuckled at that. "So, friends and family, what do we have here? Any ideas?"

It was Olga Volkov, captain of the salvage ship, Recovery One, who spoke first, addressing her comment to Jeannie's grandfather, Captain Baris of Recovery Two. "What do you think, Frank, a generation ship?"

"Sounds like it all right," he replied.

"All right, you two, what the heck is a generation ship?" asked Jeannie.

"It's a sub-lightspeed starship," replied Captain Baris. "There was a plan on Earth to build several of them before the star drive was invented. Once the faster engines were discovered the ships were converted to colonist transports.

"A generation ship is the only way to explore the galaxy if you don't have star drive. Your crew sets out on a journey to a nearby star system, but it will be their descendants who actually arrive at the destination.

"As the crew ages they have to educate and train their children to take over. The hope was to preserve the species and explore the galaxy, even though those who built the ship would never see an alien planet."

"I see," mused Jeannie. "Okay, so if that's what this object is, what do we have here, what could have gone wrong? Speculate, people."

"Could be anything, Admiral," said Olga, "mutiny, disease, anything. It's old, and if those engines just ran down then it's really old. A lot of generations could have come and gone in that length of time. Perhaps the technical knowledge to operate the ship was lost slowly over that span of time, the passengers and crew sinking back into barbarism."

"Okay, so what do we do here?"

"Admiral, if we don't investigate, I could have a mutiny on my ship," sighed Captain Ka'Ron of the Morar ship, Kreenon. "Those curious Maccay will drive the rest of us to madness."

Jeannie chuckled at that. "They truly are a curious people. Well, Ka'Ron wants to take a closer look, anybody else?"

"There might be another language or two on that ship that I could add to my database," grinned Captain Linsey da Silva, captain of the fleet's diplomat ship and Chief of Interspecies Relations.

Captain Sessas was the next to speak. Sessas, a Saurian woman for whom verbal speech is difficult, communicating mainly through a translation device created by Linsey da Silva, had risen from rescued slave to captain of the fleet's rescue ship, Retriever. She has a keen mind and is well respected by all the captains.

"Sessas curious, but wary. Sessas think Admiral curious too."

Jeannie chuckled at that. "Yes, I am, Sessas, and yet wary also. All right, we'll take a closer look. Admiral Sorenson to Probie."

"Probie is here, Admiral. There is a task for Probie?"

"Yes, my friend, there is. Outside the Reacher is another ship of unknown origins. I want you to launch and thoroughly investigate. I want to know everything you can learn about this ship."

"Probie is launching."

"The probe is away, Admiral, chuckled Captain Rhonda Moore of the Reacher, looking up from her info pad."

"All right, folks, get some rest then we'll meet here again first thing tomorrow to see what Probie can tell us." With that the meeting broke up.

* * * * *

"What is it, Tonts? Have they returned?"

"Yes, Keta, they have, but I believe there are a lot more of them than we can detect."

"Oh?"

"Yes, just a flicker now and then, but something. I just wish we had one of those intuitive elders here, their intuition would be invaluable."

"Ah yes, but they're only a few left alive, and none who have full command of their faculties. Ah well, what can you do. It was hard enough to train a young Gant before when we knew an attack was coming, now it's nearly impossible, and the world of Igen is failing.

"Do you think the outsiders will help or destroy us?"

Tonts sighed and glanced at the three entrances to the room of power. Seeing no threat, he returned his attention to his companion. "Who knows, our prophecies say it could go either way while the Growes prophecy says they will devour all. Sadly, the answer lies outside."

"Are they trying to find a way into Igen?"

"No, just buzzing about outside for now. We must wait and see; hope for the best."

As Tonts said this last, another stuck his head through one of the entrances. "Growes war party approaching."

"Dammit, Tonts, go," said Keta as she began locking the entrances. He hurried away and Keta locked the door behind her as she joined him. They dare not let the Growes get at the controls of Igen.

* * * * *

With a snarl on his face, Floo released the handle on the unyielding door. "We were so close, Eelee. So close. Did they escape again?"

"Through another opening, yes."

"And now they've sealed us off from the room of controls. They must know of the outsiders and are trying to let them in. Put out the word, every access place to Igen must be heavily guarded. All fighters must be involved." She nodded and pointed to another who hurried away to carry the orders to all Growes everywhere in Igen.

* * * * *

"Everyone's here, Admiral."

"Thank you, Vice-Admiral Drake," smiled Jeannie. "Linsey, has Probie reported yet?"

"She has, Admiral. Probie transmitted a steady stream of information to Friendship who then helped me organize much of it so we organics can understand it. Here's the basic breakdown.

"That ship is approximately ten thousand years old, is in bad shape, has a breathable atmosphere, several hull breaches that have been sealed off, and the one power source is failing. The interior is much like a planetary surface in some areas and more a ship like in others. The ship has no shields, weapons, or transporters.

"Probie also observed a small number of life signs gathering on what is believed to be a secondary bridge, but another group chased them off. She also believes that small group was aware of her and her movements. She believes the ship offers no threat to the fleet."

"Well done, Linsey. Tell Probie I said so. All right people, opinions, options?"

"Jeannie, what are we doing here?"

"Grandfather?"

"Why are we here? What are you planning to do? Are we going to pillage that ship?"

Jeannie chuckled at that. "No, Grandfather, we're not turning pirate. At the moment we're deciding if our curiosity has been sufficiently satisfied or not."

"Mine sure isn't," grinned Captain da Silva. "There has to be at least one language over there I can add to the database, and another people to meet and talk to."

Miriam Holbrooke of the Passengers Association sighed elaborately. "Linsey, you're not going to invite them all onto the Reacher, are you? Rhonda will just dump them in my lap." That brought a round of chuckles from all the captains.

"Seriously, Admiral, shouldn't we try to make contact with them, offer some help?" asked the Vice-Admiral.

"EX2 did try, Vice-Admiral," said Captain Morthel. "We got no response."

Jeannie sighed at that. "Speculate on that, people. What are the possible reasons they would not respond?"

"Could be they no longer have the functioning tech," mused Olga Volkov.

"Actually, I expect the other is the most likely reason," said Miriam.

"Miriam?"

"Admiral, you know as well as I do what happens when you have a growing population in a confined space. If we'd been left on Elysium for generations, we'd have outgrown the Caverns, some would be forced outside, others would fight for resources, etc.

"As the generations passed and education deteriorated, those remaining would slowly sink into barbarism, eventually creating a much more primitive society. The fate of the original crew of the Kreenon and their descendants clearly demonstrates this."

"Sadly, you're right, I believe, Miriam," said Jeannie. "I remember and agree, that would have been the fate of the people in the Caverns. So you believe the people on this generation ship have suffered this fate, they've devolved back to a more primitive society?"

"I think it's quite likely."

"Anyone else?"

"She's probably right, Admiral," agreed Linsey. "Probie reports all the ship's systems are on auto and in need of adjustment or repair. I'd really like to try contacting them again."

"And I'm curious as to where they came from and where they were going," mused Rhonda. "We looked at their direction of travel and see nothing back there for a long way. At their current speed they wouldn't have gotten far even in all that time, and there's nothing out in front of them except intergalactic space."

"I'm quite sure they've been moved off the original course many times over the years," said Olga.

"Tell me again they have no weapons," said Jeannie.

"They have no weapons, nor do they have shields, at least none functioning that Probie could detect," said Linsey.

"Then I guess there's no real harm in letting you have a crack at it, Linsey."

"Jeannie ..."

"Yes, my conscience?"

Frank Baris chuckled at that. "We are going to help them if we can, aren't we?"

"Yes, Grandfather, if Linsey can manage to talk to them, we'll offer to help them if we can."

"That's good to hear," he grinned, "'cause, you know, pirates wouldn't do that sort of thing."

"Grandfather, you're not supposed to tease the admiral in a staff meeting. All right, Linsey, give it a shot. Sessas, you fly back up on this one, just in case."

Don't miss out!

Visit the website below and you can sign up to receive emails whenever Prudence MacLeod publishes a new book. There's no charge and no obligation.

https://books2read.com/r/B-A-ZKBBB-QBHRC

BOOKS 2 READ

Connecting independent readers to independent writers.

Also by Prudence MacLeod

Forgotten Worlds
Suvi
Echo of the Past
Survivors
Ship
Fleet
Unite

Watch for more at https://www.prudencemacleod.com/.

Telling a story is like knitting a sweater. Start with a ball of possibilities, pull out one small thread and begin. With luck and patience you will create something quite wonderful.

About the Author

On a far off windswept island Jennifer Crandall sits with her dogs and cats creating fantastic stories for all to enjoy. She publishes as JL Crandall, Prudence MacLeod, and Jenni Leigh.

Read more at https://www.prudencemacleod.com/.